Life / { OffLine }

When the connection is lost…

By Suraj Goswami

First published in India 2014 by Frog Books
An imprint of Leadstart Publishing Pvt Ltd
1 Level, Trade Centre
Bandra Kurla Complex
Bandra (East) Mumbai 400 051 India
Telephone: +91-22-40700804
Fax: +91-22-40700800
Email: info@leadstartcorp.com
www.leadstartcorp.com / www.frogbooks.net

Sales Office:
Unit No.25/26, Building No.A/1,
Near Wadala RTO,
Wadala (East), Mumbai - 400037 India
Phone: +91 22 24046887

US Office:
Axis Corp, 7845 E Oakbrook Circle
Madison, WI 53717 USA

ISBN 978-93-83562-76-3

Book Editor: Surojit Mohan Gupta
Cover Design: Focus Design (Amit Shukla)
Layout: Chandravadan R. Shiroorkar

Typeset in Book Antiqua
Printed at Vikram Printers Pvt. Ltd., Pune

Price — India: Rs 125; Elsewhere: US $5

Dedication

I would love to dedicate this book to the dear life that has been kind enough to test, reward, and to teach me in its own unique ways and shades.

I cannot take the credit away from all my loved ones who have always stood by me and kept on instilling ever-growing faith in my first literary baby.

I still remember the tough days when, even after completing my manuscript, I was not able to make it to see the light of the day and almost gave up. It was at that time that 'my pillars of strength' gave me a strong shoulder to rest and recoup, and to keep on trying with perseverance and grit.

And last and most importantly, I can't stop thanking and going gaga about the very special one who has turned over a new leaf in life for me.

Without her, the book couldn't have made it to the publishing houses - let alone reach your hands. Thanks a ton N :)!

About the Author

Suraj Goswami is a Project Manager in the Information Technology space and Investment Banking domain by day. By night, he strives to live up to the call of his life by transforming the emotions and experiences of life into his works of fiction.

Currently based out of Pune his interests include cricket, chess, movies and reading, apart from writing.

This is Suraj's first novel which he wrote around 5 years ago. However, the turn of events on his personal front delayed the work from coming to the fore earlier.

Acknowledgements

I would like to gratefully acknowledge the thorough and meticulous supervision of Dr. Surojit Mohan Gupta during this work. I sincerely thank Mr. Swarup Nanda for the faith he has in me and my work and the careful guidance with which he has walked me through.

I can't forget the pioneering handholding and confidence boost ups which I got from Mr. Omkar Thakur through encouraging discussions. In particular I would like to acknowledge the inspiration I received from all my friends in IT space and around for sparking off the embers which eventually fired their way into the chapters of the book.

Last, but not the least, I want to thank my family and my loved one(s) for being the real pillars of strength, for keeping my faith intact, in getting my work through the stage of completion and attaining the salvation status of reaching a great publishing house.

Contents

Introduction

"IT world" -- the name has becomes so familiar that I wondered a number of times why not make an attempt to relate to the lives of so many Software (S/W) associates who eat, drink and smoke IT. I mean, why not write a travelogue or the life story of all the chaps who get "Bangalored" or "Gurgaoned" or "over-seased" some time or the other. The beauty of their lives is such an uncertain and vibrant blend of boredom, excitement, fun and exasperation that you cannot find a single word to term or define the whole saga.

This book is a simple attempt to relate and extrapolate my IT industry experiences and emotions and put them in a tale where every one of us can relate to one or the other part of it.

I have intended this book not only for all the IT associates and computer geeks but for everyone. The general image of an S/W engineer is usually projected (often in our *masala* movies and soap operas) as a nerd whose only task is of hacking other's password and invading into other's bank and other secure accounts…

The reason that I have chosen life at the onsite as the pivot of this story is because it is so very funny and peculiar. The same person with which you can have ego hassles and issues on the personal front, would be standing next to you in the kitchen, preparing the dinner with you. So many times, there is this uncanny and weird undercurrent of a cold war between you and your bosses and peers. The unique part is, you have to live with it and there is no running away from it.

Late night shifts, depression and frustration, are some side effects in disguise of this industry which one never gets to know.

The worst side effect of this business is when it makes the relationships break because of false and fragile egos, especially with your loved ones.

Well the picture is not that bad either, if not all rosy and beautiful. I have always enjoyed working in the amicable company of my friends and having long tussles with the idiot box of IT industry. The IT associates' life doesn't end only at writing stuff similar to matrix on the black screen but it spans much beyond that. It does include the vast overall global interaction which you get, and get to understand the peculiarities of the different business areas and complexities in a number of ways. There is an entire world ready to get unfolded right in front of your eyes, you just have to know what exactly you are looking for and the rest is all about making an honest effort to reach out for it.

Sounds dicey and complex? It indeed is. But the fact is, until you enjoy stepping into this world and go for a dip into the deep waters; you won't get the actual feel of it.

I hope you will love the story and, if you find it a fun book and a 'single-sitting' read, I would be more than happy with my efforts.

Happy browsing ☺!!

Chapter 1: Dreams Unleashed

"Shit"!! ... It was 6:05… I had another look at my mobile to make sure I really did it again… I cursed the traffic once again and pushed my way through the crowd to the entry gate of bus no. 729.

Delhi private buses are great examples of Indian hospitality; you are welcome anytime anywhere and in any state; no matter whether you are running, walking or sitting. You just have to wave your hand to make it stop with a screech and, when you open your eyes next, well, you have been added to the guest list. Since they are also an ardent fan of physical fitness, they never stop for you and make sure you run, sprint and then jump real hard to get inside too.

Well, in case we missed the formal firm handshakes, "Hi, I am Raj Verma, 27/m/Del... An S/W engineer in SCT and truly, madly, and happily in love with my sweetheart Nayana, who I am going to meet with now."

Please catch up with my quick jog to know me and my story in a better way…

It was another busy Friday and the streets of CP were jam packed (well they always are, in the evenings). I was just making a rough count of slaps and jabs and screams that Nayana was going to welcome me with. But it was the exciting climax of this everyday movie that used to end with hugs and kisses that always made up for the fake anger and tantrums.

I just love her.

I can never plan in my life; it simply is not in my system... I lost my watch years back and since I could do away with this need with my mobile, I never bothered to buy a new one. The clutch wires of my bike gave way 3 days back but my system is perfectly wired to delay and procrastinate perfectly to make *"Why waste fuel and add to global pollution when you have public transport"* excuses.

But still I love as this recklessness made me meet her... Whenever I think of this; it takes me down to the memory alley... It was 2 years back...

It was 2 years back when I got my first onsite assignment... The last two words are enough to trigger the adrenaline rush in the weak and one-dimensional structure of any S/W engineer who dedicates countless nights, staring at the black monitor and playing the crazy tunes on his QWERTY instrument like a zombie.

If you add the magical "long term" word to it, it gives the feeling as If you have finally hit the Jackpot, well even better ... may be the G-spot (I meant Gold by G, just FYI).

I had to drop a mail to the travels facilitator about my arrival details and itinerary. I rushed back from the office, kick-started my bike after tucking his contact details in my back pocket, and crash-landed home.

As usual, once again, I had worn one of my torn jeans, torn and loose at all the wrong places, which had no support or storage space for the items meant to be placed inside. The contact details were gone, now what?

I still relied on my memory cells and tried to recollect my thoughts, the name of the person was Nayan A. Mallikardev (then some alphabetical permutation and combinations) and it was a yahoo ID. So that would make it Nayanam@yahoo.co.in. Bingo!!!

I patted my back and immediately drafted the mail with all my arrival details. I copied to Mayank, who had been there for around a year, as well.

As my mom assisted me with the rest of the packing, the phone rang with a "no number" display. Whew, that's a quick response Mayank, I thought.

"Hey Raj! Howz life man???"

"Good Cool great … how are you … how is life … got my mail?" I was too excited to order my thoughts correctly...

"I am fine … but you would never learn to be systematic in life… Would you?"

Well, the sarcasm pinched me though he said it in a very light tone…

"Why … what went wrong man????" I felt terrible!

"You have sent the mail ID of travel guy as Nayanam@yahoo.co.in; it is actually M_Nayana@yahoo.co.in!!"

"…" I was speechless.

"Don't worry bud, Will do the needful … you carry on… Take care…"

And he hung up on me abruptly, and with a clear message that if you can't even manage yourself, how would you manage the client expectations here boss!!

I felt as flabbergasted as mixing up the names and addresses on flower bouquets sent to two girlfriends; how could I do this?

My mom, on the other hand, was busy making the multilayered architecture of the clothing and rest of the stuff in my bag. Moms always make life simple, don't they?

"Raju, should I put in more sweets for your friends?"

Friends??? Well mom, Wish you had any idea what kind of friends (?) I am going to be with.

I was still shaken by the patronizing tone of my hostile counterpart … well, I wished life could be a little easier…

My chain of thoughts was broken by another ring … now what? What did I break this time man…? Don't kill me in EMIs like this.

This time it was a local number 98104….., I relaxed and then got frustrated again, please I don't want any more credit cards and investment plans. I have enough credits and nothing to invest into.

"Hi … is this Mr Raj from SCT??" It was a lady. Smart, eh? Now they dig out the names as well along with the numbers? Well honey, here I come!! And I barked…

I just mustered all my rudeness and harshness and got ready to plant it all into my tone.

"WELL, YES, what is it about, how do you guys get the numbers or you simply take some pleasure in bugging and making pestering calls to anyone and everyone???"

I sang my own "breathless song" in one go and, with my hands on my hips, stood as if I just knocked the world boxing champion out of the ring.

"Please excuse me Sir, but I believe this time you have made an invasion into my mailbox by your meaningless mail, how do you explain that, Mr?"

Her crisp and dry voice made my shoulders droop and I quickly changed my guard into a defensive one... I just let my butts thump down on the bed.

"Well, I am very sorry, actually ... You know what ... I keep on getting ... .such annoying ... you know..."

"Whatever it is, since you accept that you did something really wrong ... can you extend me some help?"

Now it was getting confusing ... She sounded confident and unfazed by changing shades of our conversation but I couldn't figure out what she meant. I kept mum and she continued.

"My name is Nayana, I am working as a faculty in NIIT, Vikaspuri, and I am desperately looking for a job. I did my engineering 6 months back and since my college is not having a very good campus..."

Honestly speaking, I just loved listening to the sweet melody of the free flowing chain of thoughts coming from the other side; one thread leading to the other ... she sounded like a free bird, no inhibitions or compulsions, just a plain and hardcore passion to live the life to the fullest.

After she was done talking, I tried to recollect as much as possible as to what she was talking about ... Ughhhh ... I cursed myself ... but I had to say something now.

"Ok Nayana, I work in SCT and I don't know many guys in recruitment. I can just float your CV in the recruitment pool and let's hope for the best." I was content that I uttered something.

"Well, SCT is like a dream for me... It's having a global presence and, with a brand name like this, anyone would like to join the club ... please do something solid boss!!"

I felt ashamed for a moment ... here we were, who used to mock our own SCT as "Sucks at Compensation Time" and here she was, singing songs of praise and admiration for it, that too with her entry level experience.

"Well yes, you are right; I would try my level best." I just sang the parrot song.

"Ok, thanks. Keep in touch when you reach Greece and nice talking to you."

The "stay in touch" phrase from a girl always makes you feel happy and sends a chill down your spine, doesn't it? And the more the chicks, the more is the chill in life, I thought like a typical bachelor, scared of bonds and starving for all the fishes in the pond.

I was lost and wondered how she knew about my destination till I realized about the mail I had sent her. I was not at all interested in putting the phone down now, but I just happened to have a look at the time. It was already 7:15 and I had to reach the airport by 9:00.

I quickly wrapped up the call, happy that I had her number stored in my cell.

The time flew just too quickly and next moment I found myself relaxing in the waiting lounge of IGI Delhi Airport. After exchanging all the pleasantries and goodbyes with my mom (My Dad went back home soon as he became so irritated with my visa process delays that he felt sure that I was not leaving).

I was busy bombarding SMS (Small meaningless sentiments) to all my Yahoo Messenger (girl) friends, regardless of whether they bothered to even recognize who I was since I simply added them because of their nice nicknames like urspuja_xx OR sweetbu8rfly82 and … well, the list was endlessJ!

I had few of the numbers and I was just attempting to brag about the heroic voyage I was about to kick start. God must be seriously angry as all of them were picked up by unwelcoming uncles or irritating kids and the outcome was the same, I ended up cursing, getting scolded, or simply hanging up the phone.

As I was trying to see when the boarding was about to start, the little devil in my pocket rattled and rang again. I put the happy face green button, too hastily even to check the number.

The trance of a familiar charming voice started casting it spell on me.

"Hey, so have you started on your cruise Mr Raj??"

"..." Who is she ... definitely no butterfly or silvercloud from my Messenger list... But have I heard this voice before?

"Hummmm ... guess you are busy with too many hook-ups; remember me? Your travel organizer, Nayana!!!"

Oh its she again... "Hey, How did you ... oh from mail, but how come you calling so late?"

I was too happy to hide my emotions and it just splashed out of my voice ... bottom-line was; one more charming lady's contact details to flirt and show off with.

"Well I called up to wish you a very safe and sound journey dear ... and please keep in mind about my job thing ... It is really urgent for me."

"Sure, I would do that..." She sounded sweet and selfish at the same time... She did remember to wish good bye, but for her own good reason.

"...".There was a silence on the other side!

"And I would keep in touch with you... As and when I get time, I would drop a line or two to you..."

"DON'T SAY IT JUST FOR THE HECK OF IT, IF YOU WANT TO, YOU WOULD!"

The sudden transformation in her voice and the chill of the dryness of it shook me for a moment. I was walking but I came to a standstill as if someone told me "Statue".

"…"

"Look, Raj, I am sorry but I want to make good relations. They should breathe and sing and make your life alive. I don't want friends to be showcased on the cupboards of my life with the epitaphs of their manufacturing and expiry dates. I want a friend to be there for me whenever and wherever I want."

The depth and the gravity of her thoughts didn't hit the shores of my understanding which was completely choked with the dreamy fairy tales of my virtual chat world and all the butterflies and the "CoolBabe4U".

"That's ok Nayana … I would stay in touch … and sorry to have upset you."

"I hope you would Raj … now you must rush…Good night and wish you a very safe journey," and then the call got disconnected. I felt as if she was sobbing when she put down the phone. I felt an uneasy feeling inside me which I had never experienced.

From some honest corners of my non-committal mind I had a feeling that we would have some story, I didn't know how or why or what the outcome would be, but we are definitely not destined to end at this mail or call. I realized that this was bound to happen.

The rest felt like a dream to me. But Nayana did not go away from my thoughts. The beautiful and charming robotic on/off smiles of the Cathay Pacific airhostesses, the non-veg delicacies served on board, nothing could wash or fade it away. I first tried to resist but eventually just let myself dive into the thoughts of the girl who was

"N ot

A nother

Y our Hot babe

A nd

N either

A nother face in the crowd"

zzzzzzzzzzzzzzzzzzzzz…

Chapter 2: My Ship into Deep Waters

All my friends who had visited Greece earlier told me that this is an "Eye-Land" and not just an island. You cannot understand the depth and the insight of their hearty emotions till you arrive here; that too in the summers.

What is a little warm sunshine for us Indians - becomes an "Ultra high and extreme heat" for the native islanders and that is in maximum benefit of ours. The simple law of the physic (cal) sciences that states that 'the amount of concealed area of a human body is inversely proportional to the amount of environmental heat' starts looking like the best law of nature.

Soon, my eyes started landing on the smoothest of the strips and valleys as I got completely absorbed in the epiphany of "Eye-Land" moments.

Greece can be a very exciting or an equally boring place to be in; depending on your taste of flavours of life. If you love the serenity and calmness of long seashores (the sun bathing couples involved in their mushy acts are just a bonus feature), the street side cafes and restaurants which are in stark difference with the hubbubs of any tinsel town of USA, then you hit the jackpot when you land in Greece.

Well my first day in the country started with quite an eventful day. I reached there in the afternoon and was received on the El-Venizelos Airport by Sundeep.

Sundeep was there on a short-term assignment and was supposed to come back in a week after my arrival. Sundeep is quite a character. He can get real jittery and make you the same as well at times. But at the end of the day, I always find him as someone who is your best friend and would pull you out of your worst problems.

I hugged him tightly, it was great to finally see an Indian soul after 14 hours of flight; that too an old friend.

On the way from airport, Sundeep kept on giving the survival kit instructions to me.

"Raj, there are two safe ways to cross the roads here…"

"You never have to visit the interiors of Ommonia … that's troublesome."

But I just kept on giving periodic nods and rather kept myself busy in examining the fairer exhibits of my favourite physics law. The bus was air conditioned (well what a BIG change to start with) and I dozed off to sleep till Sandy shook my shoulders to wake me up with a start.

We got down at our bus stop, my gazing and serious observations had not come to a halt, so he had to literally hold my hand and make me cross the road.

We reached home, which was right above a Hard Rock Café and lounge, WoW!

103, Pangrati Square – This was going to be my home for the next 6 months to come.

The flat was real cool and why not. I compared it with my shabby flat in Gurgaon*#; where we, the roommates, virtually used be lined up on the gates of "nature call" rooms to wind up the morning chores, and I felt as I if I had risen above the poverty line … all of a sudden.

*# *The next software hub after Bangalore just in case you are not aware of this jungle of S/W and call centre robots*

Well I freshened up, not so quickly, as I enjoyed the royal comfort of the king size bath tub. I was quite unwilling to leave this comfort but the incessant thumps on the door from Sandy made me finish it sooner than expected.

I came out and tried to avoid the annoyed look on his face. I know it was quite un-cool and unacceptable for Sandy to agree to the fact that I was delaying it deliberately even though I was supposed to report to the office on that day itself.

By the time I got back after picking up the best possible attire I could choose for myself, I found that Sandy had served the food for me. The *dal,* rice and pickles tasted like ambrosia to me as I had not had good food throughout my flight. When my head and thoughts were focused completely on the meal served, Sandy broke my concentration.

"Raj, please don't think I was getting irritated as you were making me late for the office. You know me, I don't say anything even if I have to sit back late and finish others' work, I don't mind doing it."

My concentration broke and my hands stopped with my spoon half landed in the delicious depths of the Indian delicacy and my senses were not ready to detach from the sweet basmati's aroma. Still I cast a sideway glance at Sandy to ensure that he didn't feel ignored.

"No Sandy, you know I really appreciate…" But he interrupted me again.

"Raj, don't talk so formally. Does our friendship hold no meaning if we are not sitting next to each other in India??"

The underlying depths of the apparent rude statements of this guy always melted my heart and this is why I liked him so much. Leave alone harming you; he would take all the blows on himself to save you. You just have to be a little patient and understand him.

I kept mum … waiting for the real thing to come. Whenever "the big thing" was about to be uttered from his mouth, his facial gestures casted the shadow of it. His nostrils started to flutter, lips started getting parted and eyes almost got closed as if in an attempt to keep the secret from leaking out. And then it popped out.

"Raj, It's a jungle out here, please be careful, the kind of vulnerable and carefree person you are, people won't hesitate to use you and walk up the ladder of success, leaving your ass stuck in the sling."

The intensity and the fear factor of the statement first sent a chill down my spine and then did what such things always do to me, make me laugh. I did my best to hide my expressions and I tried to paint my face with hues of mock concern but it was in vain and I said.

"Sandy, at the end of the day, we are humans, not bloody S/W robots who speak in Java or C++ rather than in native Hindi or English. Why would we step over other's bodies to make our way to success? Please get a life, it doesn't work that way, what about human conscience?" I just shrugged off his warning.

"Raj, seems like you won't believe me. Well, just keep this advice at the back of your mind, like the one given by a big brother, please."

"I will mate … I definitely will, just pray I never have to plan my actions around this thought process." With this, I wrapped my arms around his shoulder and we marched towards the place where all the work was waiting, the office.

By the time I reached office, my observations of the objects of attention spread around had come down to a stagnant level. But the thirst had not been quenched.

After girls, the second fascination guys wish to ride and shake on, are the bikes. And here I saw all possible kinds of these beauties as well -- dirt, racing and cruisers -- every now and then zipping past you. Man, didn't I love this place.

"Sir, if your RADARs have locked their targets, can we move into office??"

I was really embarrassed this time as I had made Sandy really upset by the way I had kept on popping my neck out as if looking for ET forces. He was again forced to hold my hand and make me walk like a baby again. Not any more, I shook my head and controlled my thought process while we entered the office.

I had a more glamorous picture of the office portrayed in my mind. More like those shown in the movies where the hero walks in with a black leather bag in his hand, dressed in a nice suit talking to his girlfriend. Then he enters a room which is occupied by few foreigners (who sometime talk even in stupid Hinglish as well like "*Ham apka bharosa kaise karega Mr Khanna*?"). This is followed by some swift movements of the fingers on the laptop followed by some smart blabbering and the deal is done. WOW!! No wonder this is how most of the movie directors portray the S/W professionals.

I mean, I wish someone could tell them how difficult is to convince the client even for changing the case of the letter 'd' of a deal!!!. And the torture does not end here since the hero celebrates the occasion with a song and party ... well I just wish all the offices were so cool.

One more glare and a tap on the shoulders from Sandy and I hastily rushed out of my chain of thoughts.

"Man, I have really pissed him off for sure," I thought. Even then, I was not learning from the experience and once again my eyes got glued on the client office which was crammed with all the blondes, brunettes and redheads and I was just hoping to exchange glances with them.

I had to now meet with Mayank and Raghav (My boss at onsite). I thought of Raghav and felt shit scared after all the fun time I was having on the way.

Raghav; He definitely suited the title of "The tough master". If we had nothing to work on or provide the status of, he would ask, "Why can't you be proactive to take up additional responsibilities?"

...And If we followed his instructions and did something innovative and so-called "proactive", he would really be after our lives and scold.

"Do you have any idea what kind of impact the change you are making is going to have? Where is the analysis for the changes that you are making?"

Man!! I swear, "Crazy Perfectionist" is an understatement for him.

As Sandy almost shoved me into the room, I was welcomed by the familiar faces of Mayank and Raghav. Mayank was there with his usual sugar-coated warm greetings and a bear hug.

Raghav, on the other hand, started with his usual baritone voice of "Hey Raj, are you all set to give your hundred percent this time?"

"...What the F...?" What do you mean this time, when was the last time? I was baffled!! But I kept my mouth shut.

"Well, even 90 percent would do, I know 10 percent is lost in translation from Greek to English, ha haa ha."

The sick joke, followed by the atrocious laughter made the fairy memories of the outside streets swept away in a jiffy. I tried to force a smile although I could not make what the poor joke was about!

On the other hand, Mayank had already flashed his facade of yellow teeth.

Well, I thought, only if you had a tail to wag, you would have started dancing to the tunes of the song:

"My Boss is always right … My Boss is always true … I would always follow his orders … Even If I don't have a clue."

Sandy, with his typical Buddha smile, walked down and said, "Raghav, Let me start the hand over to Raj, as it is already 3:00 'o clock and I need to leave early to pack my bags."

A "Hand over Take Over" or the HOTO is more like a (My) Headache Over To (Your) Ordeal. In most of the cases there is nothing meaningful that can be handed over and the receiving party is also usually disinterested to make anything out of it. But this formality must be carried out since this is very much like morning ablutions, if you do it, fine, but if you don't, you are in for a tough time.

I was feeling fine till I sat in front of my workstation (Which I term as "Where all the work becomes stationary") and the dizziness of the long travel started to take a hold over me and I felt the whole world spinning as I tried my level best to keep my eyes open.

Sandy, who was a workaholic drunkard; was explaining to me things one by one, very methodically and meticulously. I felt like couples who get stuck in the late night-cum-early morning weddings, who just obey the instructions given by the *pundit*, impatiently waiting for the rituals to get over.

I just kept on nodding my head in simple harmonic motion every 3 seconds to convey the message that I was doing great with all the knowledge that he was transferring.

"The risk profile can be drawn out in 3 easy steps…"

"Without this factor, all data is meaningless and stupid… Bet your butt on that…"

"The heavy mail attachments get swapped by lighter HTML formats…"

"The development would take days and nights of effort … take it easy man, you have enough time."

"The thin client base ensures a global roaming access … Raghav and Mayank know it better."

"This feature ensures security against theft and hacking attacks..."

"Raj, how did you know that already…? You almost stole my words, man."

"The front end may not end up being too artistic ... Who cares anyway…?" It was bad to hear my name from him.

"QPM is the most vital assignment in the pipeline…"

With my half open and closed eyes, his talks sounded like marriage chants only, which I accepted with humble obedience. Whether I liked or not, I had to follow them.

The ceremony got over at 6:00 in the evening. I wonder how much of it I had grabbed. But I was happy and proud of my intelligence for I had recorded the entire thing on my mobile.

So I had at least stored all the valuable teachings imparted by Sandy.

"Well done Raj," I patted my back. I felt proud of myself, "kudos to you man!!"

Sandy left immediately after that, leaving me amidst the two biggies who, in between the knowledge transition session, exchanged quick glances with me which were anything but friendly.

For a moment I felt as If I was being analyzed closely like a dead mosquito under a microscopic lens and as if they would raise their placards after few minutes to declare how much I had been given on a scale of 1 to 10 after watching me perform in this short stint.

"Raj, I need these HOTO to be put in a proper document, to check your understanding," Raghav commanded me without raising his head from the monitor.

"Crazy bastard…" I murmured and cursed him under my breath.

"Did you say anything?" Now he raised his head above, trying to sniff the smokes of my verbal expletives.

"Nah, I said crazy was the bus and the road," I quickly made up some crap.

"Whatever – Finish this document by Friday, positively."

I felt sick again, was Sandy right in what he told about these guys?

I tried to force my thoughts to run on a different track and in a flash it switched to Nayana.

First I thought, "Raj what is wrong with you?? You cannot get stuck on one girl that too who is kind of selfish and talked to you just for her job. This is not you, what is happening?"

After the entire tussle in my mind, I decided to open my mails. Opening my mails after a gap of 2 to 4 days was no less than an adventure.

It indeed was a huge task of sorting the meaningful ones from the "Good Morning forwards" and "Chain mails" with the obligation of forwarding to 10 guys or else to suffer the wrath of all the gods.

As I just scanned through the list of unread mails on my monitor, my eyes got fixed on one and I just could not help smiling. It was from the young and exuberant lady who made her mark without even meeting me. This time the sender's mail ID "Nayanam@ yahoo.co.in" made perfect sense and I felt my fingers throbbing with anticipation and excitement as I clicked to open and see her mail.

It was a very short and sweet one from her. I just let the boat of my thoughts float on the waves of her beautifully woven words.

"Hi Raj! So here I am again, the travel manager, the stubborn and selfish demanding girl OR the bugging pest who till the last moment kept on instructing and asking for things. But believe me, if you think that I would feel bad about it and would mend my ways, then you are absolutely wrong. I love to be the way I am and please be ready that there would be no respite from the onslaught of my mails. Mind you, I need a reply for each and every one.

I know you are eager to hear more, but for now have this starter to boost your appetite sweetheart.

- Love,

Nayana"

Wow, I felt so good man. All my tensions and fatigue seemed to get washed away in a flash. I just stretched my arms and folded them behind my neck to let myself get lost in her thoughts. How would she look like, long hair…? No No!! The authoritative voice of her simply shows she is not like those typical "touch me not" girls. Blunt cut, big eyes ummmmm … not sure … whatever … Would I get lost in them when I stare in…?"

"Zzzzzzzzzzzzzzzzzzzzzzzzzzzzzzzzzzzzzzzzzzzzzz…"

I woke up with a start and a smile on my face. Mayank and Raghav were leaning over me like the leaning tower of Pisa.

"Hey Raj!! Too much of Jet Lag *kya*??? How'd you support in the long nights for supporting client's business, man?"

Again the sweetly wrapped sarcasm in the apparent friendly gestures hit me… I just had a look at my watch; It was 9:00 'o clock. It was time to stroll back home. Shit man, I did not even get the time to reply to her mail. First thing tomorrow Nayana, I would write back to you.

Chapter 3: Hey, it's Greek to Me

At onsite, life gets right on to track, whether you like it or not. It starts right in the morning when you start your day; trying to finish off your morning chores and find one already inside crowned on the hot (or pot) seat and the other just staring at the door to barge as the gate opens… Well you don't mind that since the locations keep on changing and someday you become the crowning glory and a waiting member the other day.

Once you learn this practical aspect of the "onsite survival kit" and are ok with it, you start enjoying the blessings of onsite. A much cleaner and healthier ambience (that makes you crib about India every time), a better sight for your eyes and definitely a marked disparity from the BEST and DTC buses to the air-conditioned buses that open as you step towards them and smoothly close behind your back.

For us, once we stepped out of the home and entered the office, life really started to run in the fastest lane. The glaring and questioning eyes of our Boss Raghav never used to leave us, even when one sneaked out for a puff or a leak. They always asked the same question, "What is the current status of the tasks assigned?"

But what really kept us busy were the requests that kept on coming from the client and the business users. We were working in the Production Support and if you don't understand what this term means, let me tell you this is an environment where the problems keep on coming like our *desi* Punjabi pop singers, every next moment you see a new one mushrooming up.

Sucks!! doesn't it??

Everyday this tough routine of ours made us stay late, at least till 9:00 in the night. By the time we were out of the office, we felt like dead men walking with nothing but our lunch boxes in our hands. Raghav, being a married fellow, used to take his bus for his place while Mayank and I used to stroll down to our flat, completely drained out of the juices of life.

Apart from all the troubles encountered on account of the culture and language being poles apart, the worst time we used to face was at the restaurant and the food junctions.

Talking and explaining to the shopkeepers what we exactly really wanted was a nightmare come true. Their reactions looked very similar to what you get back from the famous and well known neighbour country's cricket captain to any question asked in English.

Fridays used to be party time, rather I should say the "Party mood time", because it used to be the time when we could visualize ourselves sprawled on the sofa in our bare minimum attires, with beer cans on the chest and lazily watching the garrulous Greek TV programs which made no sense at all. But the very luxury of passing a lethargic weekend like couch potatoes was awesome.

We had searched and set few good English movie channels and some other ones which were way above and beyond any barriers and cultural limitations. They used to show some very educative and illustrative programs about the human body›s framework, in the very way God designed it. The individuals in those programs used to explore and show the sights of the intricacies of every nook and cranny of the anatomy; either individually or otherwise collaboratively; but we really respected and appreciated their sincere efforts and that›s why we never left a single chance to cover up the entire knowledge transfer sessions.

The concentration level used to be highest and it often led to some overflow of overwhelming emotions, never caring about the outlet it chose to vent out or the outburst of the sentiments. Keeping in mind the fact that all individuals are unique in emitting their feelings, we decided to divide the time slots for witnessing the information sharing sessions. In case you missed your slot, you had to wait for another week to watch the real action.

Whatever cribs we make for the onsite when in India and however attractive the tinsel towns of abroad may look like, the heart aches for our motherland without fail and any hint or clue that could make us catch a glimpse of India or a sniff of the Indian cuisines can drive you mad.

This is why I loved so much to go through Nayana's mails which used to be like a gush of fresh breeze; as chilled as Bacardi breezer.

Her mails used to talk and breathe the way she sounded on the phone. Initially I used to be not so prompt in responding to my mails, however later on I made it a point to get back to her on the same day without fail.

The mails never seemed to stop from either side afterwards. Every time I used to open my mailbox, I used to anticipate a new one from her and I seldom got disheartened.

Chapter 4: My Greek Weeks

It was just another day or a night of our boring rut when Mayank and I staggered back into our home and headed directly to the kitchen after donning our "Uniforms". Well, these uniforms were no typical or standard chef's dress but we used to strip to our shorts and vests (well that is one of the bare realities of the "glamorous" life).

"This Ass**** Raghu is killing us like anything, what say Raj?" he said, washing the cut vegetables in the sink.

"Yeah man!! You bet..." I was cutting the onions and felt like grabbing his hand and chopping "finger chips" out of them. In front of Raghav, he would talk in the sweetest of the melodious tones and now he was calling him "Raghu." Wow what a makeover man, you deserve an Oscar for the best con artist and nothing less than that.

"So what say, shouldn't we take the well deserved vengeance from that Son of a...?" he said, thumping the washed potatoes in the sieve.

I did not know what to say... Every word coming out of his mouth sounded to me phony and bogus, but I had to say something.

"Well, I am dying to do something like that; do you have any plans man??" I tried to play it safe; I don't trust you Mr, only God knows what version you would present to Raghav!!

"I have a very safe and sound plan to settle the scores with that R for Rascal Raghav."

I was finding it very funny but at the same time was scared and lost as well; why he is so sugary sweet in the office to him and what makes his so venomous now?

"You must be thinking why I am such a hypocrite, right? Having a different face in the office and another when away."

I kept mum and threw a defensive smile back at him. How could you read my thoughts so well, man?

"Well, you need to have double standards if you have to survive here man," he said in a philosophical manner, pouring his Black Label in the trendy glass.

I felt as if Sandy's soul just entered Mayank's body and now was speaking again the "golden words" which he had preached to me earlier. Man, is it really a jungle out here??

Please, I don't want to be here.

Apparently, I said, "You are damn right man, no doubt."

"Ok... So here is the plan ... listen to me mate."

I was all ears, to actually know how shrewd he can be in his planning.

"Do you know about the magic sheet??"

"Magic sheet!!!" The name always made it sound as if it was right out of some mysterious book of the ghosts. But actually it was a simple spreadsheet which was used to maintain the track of allowances received for the associates at client site and the expenditures made. But why is he talking about the magic sheet now??

"Yeah, but what about that; what exactly are you trying to do or plan?" I jabbered it all in one go.

"I am planning to modify that bloody shit, I mean sheet, for our own good, *beta* Raju!!" He took the last big swig and thumped down the glass on the table.

"But how would you access his machine to get to the sheet?" It was getting interesting now!

"Well, well my friend." He wrapped his arms around my shoulders as if trying to hug me. The pungent smell of the scotch (no offence meant to boozers) puffing out of his nostrils clearly showed that he had started getting the mild "kicks".

"Do you know that I have his machine's password dear??" He bragged with a wicked smile on his face which started to get contorted with the "booze effect" and the sinfulness of the plan.

"But how did you get it man...?" I was shocked at his act of perfect crime. How could he do it??

"It is easy man ... Just downloaded a freeware program from the net, installed it on his PC secretly."

"But how, he never leaves his PC unlocked, he might forget about his crying baby boy but not about his sweetheart PC." I was getting anxious and curious just to know to how he cracked it.

"Well, that was also smooth, man. One late night, after he had left, I called him up to say that there seemed to be something wrong with the programs that were running then and that my machine was not responding. So I just asked for access to his machine."

"Didn't he sulk or react awkwardly?.Because what you were saying was not very usual."

"But was very much possible, wasn't it Raj??"

"Yes..." I nodded my head like a kid. You have got some brains and blended perfectly with the hues of shrewdness. You are a perfect manager in the making, dear.

"Anyway, even if he might have spent an hour and 10 Euros to be here just to check whether I was bluffing, I would have simply said that the problem got fixed in my PC while he was on the way. And mind you, the miser Raghav would never spend 10 Euros by taxi vs. the 80 cents in bus."

"Hats off dude... You are so cool," I said, wishing someday I could be smart like him. Yes I was jealous of him at that moment.

But still I didn't know what was going on in his mind. So I asked, "But what is the plan, by the way, buddy???"

"Its simple," he rested his back on the sofa and stretched his legs on the table. "We have to access and update the magic sheet so that we get some extra bucks at this month's end." The wicked smile on his face was not ready to go away at any cost.

"WHAT?? Are you mad ... he would simply chop our heads off." My whole body was shivering at the very thought of being caught and worse, that too, by Raghav. I could visualize his thick moustache fluttering with anger and his red eyes glaring at me.

Too risky, I was scared.

"Don't be a chicken *yaar*, be a MAN!!" He uttered, gauging and reading the storms of thoughts going past my face.

Well, I bet all the guys in this world can be lured or forced to do any damn shitty thing by this inspiring (or you may say conspiring) catchphrase "Be a Man". The moment this hits the shores of our hearing senses, all men think about the embarrassment of not being a man and not about the consequences of the hole they might get dug into.

I was no exception to the above historical tradition and I helplessly gave in to it. But still the picture was too hazy to understand the blue print of the plan.

"Mayank, you need some good 20-25 minutes to carry out this stuff... He even brings his lunch and doesn't even go out ... he is a real bored to death dodo *yaar*!!!"

"Guess what? Even that has been planned out fella!!!" The smile had turned into a "I am too cool" grin now.

Now even the "J" seemed to be an understatement for my feelings. I just groped for the right words so that I didn't sound like a looser void of all the innovative ideas.

Finally I managed to mumble somehow, "And ... What ... I mean ... how would we do that?" I said "we" so it somehow looked like OUR plan and not entirely his.

"*Oye*, It's me who has taken the few sips of the scotch and it's making your tongue to stutter hero, eh!!" Enjoying every moment of the very sight of my belittlement, he posed again in his "I know it all" posture and rested his arms on the sofa. Taking a deep breath, he bent his torso towards me, as if about to unfold the "Bermuda Triangle mystery," and said

"We are going to attack his home-sick heart."

I recoiled my tensed and bent forward body back on my chair. Why does he have to dramatize everything so much? Now he stole a dialogue from *Spider man-3*.

"I don't get it Mayank..." I said, scratching my head in a failed attempt to gauge his scheme.

"You know he has been here for around a year and, moreover, has not gone to his hometown for around THREE years." He put extra emphasis on the word "THREE".

"How does it help us pal??" We cannot shift his home and all his relatives out here from India, *yaar*.

He gave me another patronizing look as if doing a "tch tch" on my intellectual abilities. Pushing his glass slightly ahead, as if forcing a checkmate with his pawn, he said, "When you are away from your country Sir, a fellow from your native place looks like the entire world to you."

"But do we know someone from his place? I don't know anyone who is from his…"

He snapped me in between. The demeaning look of his eyes had now trekked down to form his ridiculing tone.

"You know and I know that there is no one from his hometown here, but HE does NOT know." He thumped down his fist every time he spoke those words as if trying to squeeze those thoughts down the watertight inlets of my brain, which was definitely missing some crucial neurons which are quite essential for appreciating any well-crafted plan.

I kept mum… Even now I was not sure of what to say but, at least by keeping quiet, I could show that I am valuing and comprehending his plan.

That seemed to be a much better approach from my side as the rudeness in his voice seemed to soften a bit.

"So tomorrow we would decoy him into our trap by saying that there is someone we found who is from your hometown in Kerala and maybe he knows you as well.

Ok? Now that would be enough to germinate wings off his butt and he would flap them all the way to dash into the made-up character of our vivid imaginations." He said it all in one go; artistically waving his hands in the air as if Da Vinci portraying his masterpiece, "The Last Supper."

After that we had our dinner quietly, munching both on the food and our plan. Mayank, already on cloud number nine, driven by the sheer intelligence of his plot and the kicks of the Black Label swigs, quickly dozed off to sleep. I, on the other hand, apart from being hurt by the belittling act, kept on thinking about whether what we were going to do was good or bad.

I tried to force my chain of thoughts to some other direction, but it did not drift on to any other track. Shifting and turning in my bed restlessly, I could ultimately think of something very beautiful and gripping. It was about my "travel manager" alias Ms Hot and Sweet a.k.a. Nayana. Whose sweet mail was the first welcoming thing when I came here.

By that time I remembered that I hadn't replied to her mails for around a week. Well; that was way too big of an offense to be forgiven and, that too, committed against a beautiful lass was enough to issue a "must reply ASAP" warrant.

I didn't know when I dozed off into my dreams. It was a weird series of nightmares and comforting dreams that I caught sight of. First I saw I that I was falling into a deep and dark gorge, screaming and crying for help. Then a long way deep down, when I had lost all the hopes of any support, there came an angel face, stopped me from falling, and carried me all the way up to the sunshine.

But the sunshine faded again and I found myself caught in a hell with demons all around pulling me towards the infernos ablaze all around me. Again my cherub rescued me out of the tortures and embraced me, all the way up to the clouds.

I woke up late; with a heavy and spinning head. I was feeling dizzy and confused. What were the dreams all about? Unfortunately, there was no time to get upset or give them any thought to. Quickly I got ready and boarded the bus with Mayank. I had almost forgotten about the plan we had to execute, so as soon as I recalled it, I kick started the discussion again.

"Are you very sure we are going to do this, man??" I turned my face and asked.

"Why not ... we have already finalized it, right?" His face was much calm and having an officious aura which I somehow hated. It looked like an ugly and fake face camouflaged under the smiley mask.

"..."

I had nothing to say so I just sat straight again and started staring in the far.

As if fathoming my thought process, he said, "Cheating a cheater is not cheating at all, dear!!" He said in a chilled voice, pursing his lips tightly.

I kept mum ... knowing that more of this lecture was yet to come. It did come indeed.

"See Raj, these allowances come for us eventually; that Hitler sanctions only the pimples out of the complete pack. What does he keep the rest for, his *Idli sambar* shop may be?"

Now it made a little sense to me. Maybe he is fooling the man who deserves to be. But by then I had triggered the eruption of a suppressed volcano and the lava was blistering hot, indeed.

"He keeps us like chained dogs, even worse since we are not even allowed to bark back or bite. The only thing keeping me here is the enticing clinking of the foreign currency coins. So if life is turning out to be a complete bitch and we HAVE to live like dogs, then why not screw back the life the way it deserves to be?"

His face had turned completely red with overpowering emotions and anger. I just pressed his shoulders and sat back quietly.

For the rest of the way, none of us uttered a single word.

After alighting from the bus, we quickly finalized the name of the non-existent entity we had planted the very last night. I suggested "Raja" as the name of the character but he again won the race by suggesting "Swami" and illustrated how it was the best choice by quickly suffixing it with Rama, Bala and Guru to fabricate three varied specimens and I had to agree to it. This time I actually admired his swift thinking since he said that we'd entrap Mr Hitler by saying that we could hear only the swami part of the name.

We entered office quietly and, as usual, found the big boss zipped and locked in his seat with his head almost buried in the monitor in sheer concentration as if trying to break the DNA code for the Genome project. We wished him a good morning and parked ourselves into our seats without expecting a reply. We knew that when he was busy or pretended to be busy like this, the "Good Morning" wish would echo back from his "don't disturb" firewall without any effect.

After booting our machines up and running, Mayank quietly dropped the bomb.

"Raghav, you know someone from your hometown called ... some 'Swami', we met him at the metro station."

No response.

It felt as if his words were some space shuttle launched from NASA to MARS that would take few days to land there.

When we almost felt that our plan had turned out to be a fiasco even before starting, he calmly darted back in a sarcastic manner.

"Do you talk to every Indian or Asian passing by you?"

'We are gone and gone for good.' This is what I could think about the whole situation. All of a sudden our whole plot seemed to be like a stupid and baseless one to me. Why would anyone fall for it?

Next few minutes felt like an eternity to us. Just when we felt like we had lost the battle, he got up from his seat and said.

"Where did you meet that guy? Did you say the name was Lingaswami?"

By this time, Mayank, obviously scared, had gone back into his cocoon and was staring at the monitor in mock concentration. I knew he was just checking his mails yet pretended as if he was trying to crack the Da Vinci code.

I didn't let this opportunity go off and quickly replied, "No Raghav, I am not sure of the complete name but definitely some swami. Do you remember, Mayank, by any chance?"

Mayank, I guess, too surprised by my witty response, lifted his head up in a manner that reminded me of an innocent cow lifting its head up while grazing. Wow, one more Oscar goes to you!!!

He slipped his hands into his trousers and we knew that he was ready to move. We were familiar with the fact that he hated leaving his lovable office and sweetheart machine like this but whenever he had to do it, he used to make it look like an inevitable event.

"Guess it is someone needing my help and maybe it is someone who knows me, so I should go, right?" He was trying his level best to justify his stand.

We did not say anything apart from the approving nod of our heads. By that time we had become experts in the art of showing the "dead busy state" even if doing the most meaningless web surfing or chatting.

The moment he left, we quickly sprang to our feet and took our positions. I stood at the main gate to keep an eye if any one appeared at the other end of the lobby, whereas Mayank was right on the money. Opening the spreadsheet and doing the modifications here and there.

He was done in the next 15 minutes and quickly we took the weights off our feet to get back into our chairs again, too excited to sit quietly.

"How much...?" I asked anxiously, trying to gulp all the excitement down my throat.

"50 Euros each." He said, suppressing his smile, not sure when the devil would enter the room and not sure in what kind of a mood.

"50 is neat, man." I quickly calculated all the luxuries that we could afford with these bucks and the choices were many. I just could not help smiling as the guilt of the misdeed had vanished long back ... after the "Eye for an eye" preaching from Mayank.

It was another good 20 minutes before Raghav sauntered down the room, astonishingly, wearing a smile on his face.

This actually sent a chill down our spine, what actually he is hiding in his devilish mind?

Mayank started to speak something but he ended up only clearing his throat.

Silence is the best statement when in doubt or scared.

"I could not find Linga today but landed into the corner shop which turned out to be owned by someone from my hometown. Thanks guys."

Sometimes a shot in the dark proves to strike the best possible deal when your luck is really on a high.

I hummed a melody from an old Hindi Dev Anand movie. For the first time in the day, I felt relaxed as the mission was accomplished successfully. But I felt something was seriously missing.

I opened Nayana's unread mails for the day and started reading them quietly, so that her magic could overpower my agitated thoughts.

Today it was an enchanting poem written by her

"Nayana Malhotra" <Nayanam@yahoo.co.in@ yahoo.co.in> 05/25/2006 14:21 IST	To	"Raj Verma" <Raj_Verma@sct.com>
	cc	
	bcc	
	Subject	Silent Prayer

Silent Prayer

When the nights are long and even the hush is the sweetest song,
This is when we head for the path, where we have been along
Don't say a word, let the dewdrops fall...
Let the eyes do the talking, the hearts get it all!
Because the time passes swiftly, and such moments are rare
So I wish you to be with me, is my silent prayer!!!

Going through the poem, I could feel as if I was walking along the seashore with her beneath a start-studded sky. Such mails make your day beautiful, don't they?

My thoughts again got drifted away from the work.

"There she is, so innocent and pure. What does she think of me, a simple and straightforward guy? Someone, who can be trusted; is honest and truthful…,

And here I am, being an accomplice in hacking password, stealing money…

Am I becoming another beast of the jungle?”

I groped inside my conscience to find the answer. There was no response, and I could hear only my questions coming back and the never-ending echo.

Chapter 5: The Naked Truth

Greece, apart from the above incentives, had another added bonus which no other US and UK onsite can offer and that is the fact that our languages are "Greek to each other". We had the liberty of uttering the most generous eruptions of emotions which used to come straight out of our hearts at the very sight of the beautiful lasses walking past us. We had the choice of both English and Hindi; however we preferred to go with the latter as it is closer to our hearts and gives more room and space for our freedom of expressions.

Then one fine weekend, we saw our wild thoughts prompting us to some real action.

It was another such Friday evening when we closed all the unfinished business for the day and were trying our luck with navigating and searching for some generous websites believing and approving the liberty of passionate thoughts. And the delight of it was emitting from all possible pores of my face. Mayank, on the other hand, was still deciphering his Da Vinci Code, although doing the same stuff as me. On Friday evenings, we had another reason to celebrate since Raghav used to be in a real chilled out mood and Mayank and I kept on winking at each other enjoying the tapping of his shoes and the whistling and the muttering of some hit South Indian songs.

As we were about to leave, after picking up our lunch boxes, Mayank walked down from his seat and stood between Raghav and my seat, with an unfathomable smirk on his face as if Lord Krishna were about to unfold the darkest and complex secrets of KARMA and eternal truths of life and death.

"What is it Mayank??" Both Raghav and I barked at the same time, driven really annoyed by the way he was making us wait for whatever novel idea he was about to coin and present.

"Chill guys, I am about to tell you about the philosophical truths of life and you are shunning away from it!!".He uttered, with both hands spread in the air, as if addressing a big election rally.

"Cut the crap Mayank... Tell us what it is all about." Raghav's baritone voice resonated the whole room as he switched off the PC and stood up to go home.

"Do you know why we dress up in so many boring clothes?" He questioned us with such a grave face, as if he was about to save humanity from an alien attack.

I seriously doubted whether Mayank had started boozing during office hours as well. I stepped closer to him to sniff it with my nostrils. But there was not even a faint hint of vodka or scotch.

"You need some rest, dear!!" Raghav patted his shoulders patronizingly as he put his hands in his pockets, ready to move!

"And you I and all of us just need to relax and pay heed to what I am saying." Mayank's expressions were still unfazed.

What exactly was he trying to prove? I just hoped that he was not feeling too much at fault because of the magic sheet manipulation and his guilty conscience was just making him behave erratically. I was very much concerned for my ass as well but then I could just listen to him.

"We are hypocrites and that's why we dress up so much. We are afraid of accepting the bare realities of our bodies. But the primal instincts and our urges force us to be in our natural nudities whenever we feel free of our mortal inhibitions."

Well, to a certain extent I do agree chap, but all the way, I am so sorry. I just tried to visualize it and the very idea of me and Mayank cooking in the primitive states in the kitchen was atrocious.

Raghav, on the other hand, gave him a look, which showed that he was very well aware of the whole melodrama. He just folded his arms over his chest and said, "Tell me fast, what the bottom-line is, dear??"

Mayank blinked his eyes and slowly combed his hair back with his fingers. I knew that expression; he was about to explode all the tensions that he had built up in the room so far.

....

"We are going to a strip club tonight!!!"

"WHAT?" Again Raghav and I yelled in unison. Raghav's feet stopped as if he had stepped on a land mine and just couldn't move.

What a waste of time and energy, *yaar*. Has he gone mad?

"Guess it's you who needs some rest?" Raghav said and approached the door.

"But give me a good reason why we can't relieve our stressed bodies and mind??"

Mayank, what are you doing man ... please keep mum; at the end of the day, he is our boss, for God's sake talk sense.

Raghav looked really annoyed by now. On surface he said, "I am married and a father as well."

"But we are men at the end of the day; anyway we are not going to be there for fornication. We came, we saw, and we left. What is wrong in that?"

Had Caesar been alive today, he wouldn't have waited for Brutus to kill him after hearing such cheap use of his victorious remark, rather he would have done the honours himself after saying "You too Mayank."

I tried to add a new viewpoint to the whole discussion by saying, "What if the police catches us, what to do then?"

"They can't catch us and publish our photos in the newspaper since these clubs are completely legal." Mayank tersely retorted.

Frankly speaking, I had already started liking the idea but was feeling too shy and timid to express my wild desires.

There was a silence in the room that persisted way too long. Mayank was standing tall like a Brave heart; Raghav was not any more resistive of the proposal but definitely pondering over the pros and cons of the situation.

I, on the other hand, was very much in for the offer and controlled myself not to start drooling at the very thought of what we would get to see if the proposed idea was accepted unanimously.

Raghav broke the ice eventually, "So can we meet at 12:00 at the metro station?"

I did my best not to flash the close up shine of my broad teeth.

"I know the venue so this won't be a problem." "Sharp at 12:00 'o clock, then?" Mayank queried, as If checking if any of the brave men would retreat at the last moment.

"Please don't tell Sudha about it, I won't be able to face her if she gets to know," Raghav requested.

I felt angry at the stand of this pseudo-family man. If you love your wife sooooo much, why do you to fall for the sleazy pleasures.

"Positive Raghav, just between three of us!" Mayank gestured by zipping his lips closed with his fingers.

After that we quickly separated and Mayank and I rushed back home to get ready for the pleasure ride.

I took all my time in the bathroom under the shower and to get ready as if I was going to do the main performance at the club. Mayank, on the other hand, again looked like a smooth operator; effortless and suave.

"Mayank, why do we need Raghav to accompany us, he is such a boring fellow. He is going to kill all the excitement." I cribbed, drying my hair with the towel.

"Look at the brighter part of the story, if anything goes wrong; at least the blame would be shared by three of us and not by the two of us only." He analyzed it like the director of the planning commission.

Wrong!! The word itself sounded very wrong in itself. What all can go wrong if we go to the club? I let my imagination loose to cover all the diverse possibilities from being thrown out by the bouncers to the worst outcome of catching AIDS.

Mayank was still lost in his planning while rolling up the sleeves of his designer party shirt. He was in his own flow of thoughts and then he gave them words.

"He is a senior guy, here for around three years or more. His credibility and level of maturity is way too better than us. In case of a crisis, he can save our ass. And If the boss himself is with us, then why should we be worried about getting caught."

Makes sense!! Anyway I was not in a mood for any further discussion and then we made our way out of home, heading directly to the metro station.

"And there is one more thing that would make us even more happy," Mayank said, smiling back at his own reflection in the mirror of a shop on the street.

"What ... what is that...?" I had no idea what he was talking about.

"What better use can we make of the 50 Euros that we stripped him off?" His defiant grin refused to go.

The air echoed with our broad chuckles and we headed to our destination after a high five.

We met Raunchy Raghav at the metro station; he was bawdily dressed in a red shining shirt and tight jeans.

"Elvis Presley." Mayank whispered in my ear and I could hardly suppress my smile as I immediately visualized grossly dressed Raghav with a guitar hanging on his neck, studded with blinking and twinkling tiny lights all over it.

Quickly we made ourselves comfy in a cab and asked the cabbie to take us to the Sygrou area where all the "do the undo act" clubs were located. All the way we kept on smirking and tapping our feet with great expectations.

The cab came to a halt with a screech in front of the "Dil_"O" Palace". The driver winked at us with a wickedly flashed smile as he pointed his fingers at the twinkling lights all around the hoarding which flaunted the outline of a curvaceous chick relaxing in a very compromising pose.

We got down from the car, our bodies almost clutched with each other and we kept on nudging and hinting each other to make a move forward. Eventually Mayank moved ahead, mustering all his strength.

There was an aged man standing outside the club, clad in a very nice and shining business suit and till the time we got him close enough to be within our earshot, we did not know that he was a guy from the club itself making very enticing statements about the assets (and no liabilities) of the lasses who were doing jigs inside.

We almost got swept off our feet as we actually gave colours to our imagination to his tempting words and quickly found ourselves crash landed on the reception desk. The guy on the reception quickly ran us through his orientation program to enrich us with all the shades of delights and distractions.

By this time, Mayank had become quite easy and upbeat, so he just asked the guy at the reception,

"How much for the entry fee and can we have a peek inside before we go in?" We were surprised at the way he confidently spoke about it.

"Oh *Ser* (Sir), Only 20 Euros!! You *khan* surely go inside and see da beautiful girls, but one time only one," his deformed English fell from his mouth like the rubbles of an old construction.

"Raj, you go in and see if it is worth the bucks," Mayank whispered in my ears.

His words made me spring back to my feet in grave attention, from my relaxed and slumped position on the reception desk. I felt like the soldier on the front, being ordered to venture out and check the vantage positions of the enemy.

"Why me?" was the first question that I was forced to ask but kept mum since I felt like a brave heart, carrying the huge expectations on my shoulders.

I stepped ahead, as the leather cushioned door was opened for me ... and I entered a new world.

It was an aroma of expensive perfumes blended with the sight of blue and hazy smoke that enveloped the whole scene. It took me undertaking some squinting exercises till I could adjust my eyes to the pitch darkness. I could see the spinning discotheque wheels that threw multihued zebra stripes on the spectators.

As only my head was stuck in the cavern, doing the surveillance, I could imagine the state of mind of Mayank and Raghav, anxiously waiting for my status report to be out.

By then I had finished my acclimatization act and set my eyes on one of the performers who was roaming around in a satin white dress, flashing a contagious smile to everyone and planting a soft peck on the spectators seated here and there.

I silently stalked her path as she moved around; placing her arms around her admirers and making them sip their drinks with her tender hands.

"C'mon, walk out of this boring gear sweetheart," I placed my silent prayer to the Venus, the Greek Goddess of Love.

But to my frustration and despair, she happily kept on performing her welcome act on and again.

I pulled back my head from the "peeping tom hole" and pulled a long face.

Let's get back guys, I secretly gestured with a wink and we quickly made a discussion huddle as we came out of the club.

"What's the matter?" Mayank asked, disappointment pouring down from every part of his face.

"It's not value for the money guys." I declared as if reading out the five year planning and policy page as a cabinet minister in front of dissatisfied opposition party members.

"But ... why ... I mean what is so bad in there?" Raghav turned and paced up to be with us as we started to walk back home, with unwilling heavy legs.

"See, that is the problem, there is nothing bad going on inside, because for us, bad is good tonight, right??" I tried my best to crack this philosophical joke.

Nobody seemed to appreciate the beauty of my statement, rather gave me an annoyed look, to gouge the truth out of me.

"Ok, ok, let me tell that there is no strip dance going on inside, it's all fake and bogus." I let my hands open in the air, like a monk, whose Bentley got stolen even before he rode it.

"..." No reaction. "Carry on Raj..." the glaring eyes said.

"I kept watching a girl inside the club; she was clad in a white dress, happily moving around but did not strip even her hanky from her waist band."

"What actually was she wearing, Raj?" Mayank darted back.

"A white and red frock kind of dress and..."

"...and a white cap as well??" Mayank stopped me midway with his counter question.

"...Yes ... How do you know...?" I was baffled ... I stared at Raghav's face which was flashing a quiet smirk now.

"Did you see what was going on the centre stage?" Raghav asked in a chilled voice.

Oops!!... I simply forgot to see that in my James Bond act of tracking and focusing only on one subject. I nodded my head in the negative.

Next thing I knew was the onslaught of abusive language (blessing all my relatives) and spanking placed all over my shoulders and back.

"You assssss..." Mayank yelled at the top of his voice, "All you could spot there was a WAITRESS, out of all those hotties????"

For a moment, I wished I belonged to the ancient age of Lord Rama and there could be a landslide to give me a place in the comfy lap of Mother Earth.

But nothing of that sort happened and I stood amidst the screening eyes, my head buried in my chest and hands behind my back, waiting for the rope to be pulled.

It was midnight by that time and we were half way down to our home, really not knowing what to do.

"There is another club closer by, if we take the next left from the metro station." I tried to save my ass in the makeup act.

"Let's go there..." Mayank and Raghav barked in unison.

We marched ahead to our next destination, the new fort to be conquered.

The new fort was named "Tit for tat". It had the same look and feel apart from the fact that the girl portrayed on the hoarding was in a different tempting pose.

We were too quick to enter the club this time, not regretting about the money as "this part of the night was sponsored by our caring and loving Raghav."

We entered and I rectified my earlier blunder by spotting the dance stage right in the centre. There we saw a tall and slender beauty, clad in a Santa Claus red dress and a Snow White cap. She was shaking and rocking her assets in the most sensuous manner.

Our and the rest of the lusty eyes nearly popped out when she started shedding her attire, peeling them off slowly. All the tables being packed, we got no seats to have a nice look at the centre stage beauties. It was kind of uncomfortable initially but as few of the beautiful damsels passed by us in their flimsy see-through robes, our comfort indices hit an all time high.

As the seats near a centre stage got empty, we nearly jumped to those seats as if playing the final round of musical chair. As and when we got seated our drinks were quickly served.

There came the expert's comment from Mayank, "See you have to take very very little sips from your drinks. This is the free one and if you finish it fast, it would be very awkward to sit with drooling eyes and empty tumblers!!!"

We silently nodded our heads and just kept on soaking our lips without gulping down even a drop of it. It was not at all a problem as our thirsts were getting quenched in a different and effective manner.

After another steamy dance of "Airhostesses", that kept our eyes glued to the stage, we took our glances back on each other; it was an absolutely hilarious scene that tickled all our funny bones.

We had seen Raghav crushed under heavy work load and pressure of client meetings. But this time it was a gorgeous and scantily clad seductress who was seated in the crossed legs lap of Raghav and his hands were awkwardly placed on her waist and knees.

"Would you buy me a drink, sweetheart?" she said in a husky voice, running her fingers on Raghav's forehead where he had started sweating profusely.

"Ah ... eh ... Can I go to the washroom...? Will be back in a flash" He stammered and sprang up to his legs, almost throwing the girl on the round table and ran away inside.

We had cupped our hands on our mouth, pretending to cough and choke. But the moment he left, we broke into hysterical laughter, not knowing how to control it.

"What an ass****" the chick grunted with mock anger, with her hands on her hurt hips.

"We do agree with you, lady...," we said in unison and raised our glasses, mimicking a Cheers act!!

Raghav took longer than anticipated and when he came back, he looked more anxious than earlier. His ears had turned red as if someone had hung himself from them.

"We need to be back on our way, as soon as possible." He sounded really frightened, as If he had met some ghost inside.

"Marco is here, I found him with one of the dancers in the bathroom ... how can he do all that...?" His nostrils were still swollen with excitement and disbelief.

Marco was head of the team of the business users in our bank. Although he was a jovial and cheerful man, we never expected him to be in a strip club.

"Calm down Raghav, we cannot go back home now; we cannot get a taxi easily at this time." Mayank raised his concern. Although we knew that getting a cab was not going to be difficult at all.

But the trick worked. We convinced Raghav to stay in for few more hours as we were in no mood to leave without any real action. Anyway Raghav was off the "wanted list" now since the girl who got pissed off by Raghav, gestured all her "union members" not to even hover around him.

A lanky babe started approaching me; her never ending legs carrying her well honed torso with a lot of wiggles and wobbles. I really felt bells starting to ring in my heart. But this ring sounded familiar and I felt it coming from my trousers. Before I could think that something was seriously wrong with my organic system, I found that it was my mobile that was abuzz and nothing else.

Reluctantly I opened the flap and found it was "Nayana Calling" flashing on the panel.

"Couldn't you find a better time to call me up Nayana?" I murmured as I helplessly watched the blonde turning on her heels and walking away, showing me her curvy bare back.

There was no point feeling irritated as one in hand is always better than the one in another's lap. Boosted by my optimistic thinking, I walked out of the club and hit my happy face green button.

"Hi Raj ... How are you doing there?" in came the voice that gushed in like a fresh gust of cool air.

"I am fine ... doing good Nayana..." I tried my best to hide the restlessness in my voice, tapping my fingers on the bonnet of a cab.

"So how is the office and everything?" Her voice sounded drowsy, as if she hadn't slept for long.

"Everything is great here dear." I felt puzzled as she definitely intended to ask something other than what she pretended to.

"When are you coming back ... Raj?" Her voice seemed to be coming from some far-off point, fading off every moment.

My quickly moving feet, that were pacing up and down, came to a halt. There was always an element of uncanny mystery in her voice, this time it was very deep and grave.

"Are you all right Nayana...?" My thoughts got completely drifted from the hustle and bustle of the pub.

"I am missing you Raj … I want you back here…" She broke into a hysterical sobbing all of a sudden.

I tried hard but couldn't understand the sudden outburst of her emotions and I just tried to console her. Usually a guy like me would have tried to take advantage of her and invade in her personal space. But she sounded so vulnerable that I did not feel like playing any games with her.

I talked to her for the next one hour till she calmed down a bit and we wished each other good night and hung up.

The night was not as good inside the club when I walked back in. Raghav was still hiding in his cocoon while Mayank was fuming and glared at me as if I had walked out of the parliament when he badly needed the vote of confidence.

"Oh … back so soon!! I thought you were going to put all your girlfriends to sleep." He cribbed tersely.

I tried to show as if nothing had happened so far. I asked innocently, "How is it going on Hunk??" gently tapping Mayank's knees.

"Well I am having a ball out here… Don't you see that all the girls are dying to give me a hug," Mayank sulked, gritting his teeth hard and glanced sideways; gesturing me to have a look at the corner.

Then I realized why Mayank was desperately looking for me to come back soon. In that corner, I saw a bunch of lasses standing who were taking twenty Euros from each of the clients and taking them inside.

"What's happening in there, man?" I asked Mayank, my mouth was open in awe, big enough to give way to an Airbus-380.

"Boss, that's the real fun, this is where you get a personal dance for you, for twenty bucks," Mayank uttered, trying his best not to drool out his overpowering emotions.

I was hesitant to move ahead but pushed by Mayank's nudges and my own primal desires, I found me and Mayank standing in the same corner after five minutes.

We slipped our hands in our pockets to take out our wallets, without moving our gaze from the bunch of the beauties around to lock our targets. This was the time when the phone rang again.

"Damn, Nayana, what's wrong with you?" I mumbled and cursed.

"Relax baby, that's mine...," Mayank tapped my shoulders, without taking his eyes off from a tall and pretty Russian girl.

"Who is calling, at least look down." I got really annoyed as his gaze got almost fixed on her.

His facial expressions of rainbow changed from coloured to black and white and then to complete pitch dark.

"It's a call from the office." He said meekly. "Something has failed and the client needs this to be fixed in next two hours"

The rest felt like a nightmare. We towed our feet away from the place and felt like kids, taken to the candy shop and then dragged all the way back home, worse, maybe even to school.

Raghav was more than willing to get away from that place.

We got back from the office early next morning after fixing the problem.

Chapter 6: The Proposal

If you ever regret the fact that you never had a chance to watch a French Open final at the Rolland Garros, then you are very much welcome as a spectator to a meeting between Raghav and the clients. You would be made to sit right between them, right in the VIP box kind of place. Rest assured, as for the entire meeting you would be swivelling your head from left to right watching the entire ball game from one court to the other.

Even when I tried to say something in those meetings, he would just gesture with his hand towards me to keep mum. Actually I preferred to stay silent only, since his reactions to anything said by me used to as bad as if a stray street dog made the offence of barking at a German shepherd coming out of a bungalow.

Anyways, it was the Monday morning after our action packed Friday night after which we were really stirred and visibly weak in our knees. We were so shocked that we all kept mum and really didn't know what to talk about, apart from the occasional smiles and nods of the heads.

At 11:00 'o clock, by the time, life had come back to the normal track to a certain extent, the broadcast from AIR (a.k.a. Always Intimidating Raghav), woke us up from our slumbers.

"Guys, let's go to the meeting for the QPM," and without casting a glance at us, he marched past us.

"Rasc..." Mayank was halfway down his insulting act without realizing that he was still within Raghav's earshot.

"You said something, Mayank...?" Raghav was quick to react as he turned back on his heels.

"Rasp ... Raspberries ... Raghav did you taste the raspberries from the square kiosk shop??" Mayank's face looked like that of a teenager surfing smut websites and caught red handed by his dad in the middle of the night.

"We had enough of the exciting berries last Friday night Mayank; let's do some boring work now," Raghav said in a cautioning and caustic tone and ventured out.

Mayank was left sulking, yet he completed the ritual by muttering the last few words in Hindi; later on when he had left the scene.

As we entered the room for discussion, we realized that Raghav had already started the discussion with Xenia Papadopoulos. (The name for which we gave great trouble to our tongue and mouth and even after that could never pronounce it correctly).

Had this been any other meeting, we could have easily buried our heads into the proposal document, prepared, reviewed and finalized by Mr Raghav. But this was a different case altogether. It was the ambitious and prestigious initiative in the domain of Investment Banking. Anyone would have liked to lay their hands on it and have a complete hold over it.

Raghav always taught us that good proposals should be like mutual fund investment plans. Client should be easily enticed to buy the ideas and offers proposed but by the time he realizes the minuscule characters of "Terms and Conditions", it should be too late.

As the meeting progressed, it was the usual ball game between the client and Mr "I know it all". We took our inputs and quickly jotted down the critical points in our notepads.

Throughout the meeting, he kept on gesturing like a traffic police inspector to show red lights for all the potential inputs coming from our side.

In the other meetings, neither of us cared a damn about what happened but, because of our great concern over this esteemed issue, we were forced to keep our eyes open.

Since this was the first time that I had paid close attention to Raghav's presentation abilities and articulateness, I found that he was impressive. The pause and the right gestures of his hands seem to direct the flow as per his will. No doubt the client loved him like hell.

"There is a serious problem with QPM that we have still not covered, Marco!!" Raghav declared … resting his back on the seat.

"Hey Raghav, don't be so honest, man..." I quickly thought, not really appreciating this sincere move from his side.

"What exactly is that, Raghav?" Marco got really worried as he bent forward to take a sip from his espresso.

I tried my level best to get Mayank's attention by winking secretly at him. I desperately wanted him to nudge Raghav so that he could curb his confession act. But, as usual, I found him establishing remote connectivity with Cynthia, the blue-eyed girl who had joined the bank two months back. Hopelessly, I brought my focus back to the discussion.

"This is going to happen in case we come across a situation where we need to ensure data authenticity in cases it is not received from a secure source." Raghav said crisply.

"Deciphering – Encrypting..." I just loved these concepts and I almost started fidgeting in the chair like a kindergarten kid to raise my hand in the air and answer.

"But we have all the secure sources currently who are giving us the input feeds." Marco said coolly, exhaling puffs of white smoke rings from his Cuban cigar.

"Ok then we exclude this point from the proposal. Great!!" Raghav announced.

I breathed a sigh of relief; Raghav had almost screwed it by suggesting the lacuna in the design and architecture, even before the proposal was to be prepared.

The meeting finished on this note and we walked down the stairs. I paced up with the 'Racing Raghav' and cribbed like a kid.

"Why did you have to tell about the loopholes of the solution, that too to Marco?" I did my best complaint act, doing everything but thumping my feet on the ground.

"You know shit about proposals Raj... You need to grow up," Raghav barked back at me.

The Rough Raghav was at his best "Ring master" act. The key to learn from this man was to shrug off all the humiliation or to take it as 'starters' before he offered the main course.

I quietly kept on walking ... waiting for his anger to subside.

"See Raj!!".Finally he spoke the golden words, chewing his lips. I knew some big disclosure was coming up.

"Do you remember that this point about information security was mentioned in the contract?" He questioned.

"Yes I do Raghav." He was making sense; that is why he had floated it in the meeting.

He flowed along with his theory. "And you know that how relaxed and laidback kind of a person Marco is?" He pulled up his sleeves slowly as if munching on his thoughts.

"Yes." I could vaguely make the connection but was not really sure how he was going to craft the perfect finish.

"So now I would put it in the document for records and float it across through mails to everyone in client and SCT management team."

Wow ... and then even if this issue crops up anytime, we can easily put the ball back in their court, saying that we tried our best to take care of this, yet it was not suggested to be implemented.

"You are a genius Raghav." I sent this silent expression of admiration to Raghav by widening my eyes and he gracefully accepted it.

"Would you like to prepare the presentation of the proposal for this, Raj?" Raghav asked me as if he could read my frustration of not having done anything significant so far.

It was a dream for me. The proposal document is the Bible and the foundation for all the design and development work to follow. At my level, it was my passion to join the league of managers and senior executives.

I nodded my head, not actually believing what I was hearing.

"Ok, let me see when can I sit with you to give you some tips and sample documents, ok?"

I felt so happy the first time in all these months that I just wanted to yell "Hats off to you, Ravishing Raghav."

Suddenly Mayank rushed into the room, excited and all smiles.

"What is the good news Mayank?" Raghav quietly asked, obviously unhappy with the way he was jumping around.

"Nothing Raghav..." His giggle and spark disappeared like the IT jobs that vanished after the bubble of dot com busted.

"No, nothing Raghav..." He quietly sat on his chair.

Later on, when I caught him in the canteen, he told me that he had taken the cell number of Cynthia and was planning to go on a date with her the very next weekend.

I guess he got a better deal signed off.

Chapter 7: A Page from Raghav's Diary

Hi, I am Raghav K. A. Shastri; I won't tell you the full expansion of the abbreviated form since then you might possibly loose all the interest because of the complexity of it. Jokes apart; I very well know that I am amicably called Rascal or Rogue or "Raunchy" by my colleagues Raj and Mayank. As a matter of fact, I just love it.

It is not because I love donning the robe of a rough 'n tough "ring master" and make them run all around for no good reason. There is an old and long story behind that.

It was around four years back when two of my friends, Krishna and Hrishi, joined at the same client site and for the same project as the current one. The team was headed by an exuberant and young fellow whose name was Rajeev. A not so old guy as usually most managers are. For the ease of the narrator, that's me, let's call this cheerful lot as the "Team".

Onsite coordinators are like the changing Chief Ministers of our Indian states. Whenever a replacement takes place, the old policies go for a toss and there is a paradigm shift in the guiding principles.

Being on top of things and having a good command are bare minimum essential requirements for the managers as taught by any Management Guru.

Rajeev was an exception to this rule. Driven by his own ideology and individual high-soaring approach towards life, he overhauled the autocratic approach into a democratic one. Everyone in the team started going to the client meetings, began to have a say in the decision making and opinions that gave a fresh look to the air at client site…

The attitude did not die out within the four walls of the office. Be it a late night movie, a discotheque at the downtown or an all night boozing at the "Rocking Studs" Bar, the team always stayed together and enjoyed together. The motto was:

"The team having blasts together; lasts together!!!"

It was all going fine till one day the carefree approach became way too careless.

Greece, like many other countries in the world, is vastly hit by the problem of illegal immigrants. The majority intake comes from Asian countries of Pakistan, Bangladesh and a little bit from India as well. The rest of the lot is from Albania, Spain and China, etc.

It was one Friday evening when the hang out gang was sauntering back from their booze and let the legs go loose party when they ran into Jasbeer.

Jasbeer was quite a character. He migrated from Punjab when he was eleven (Now even that was not a reliable piece of information). Team was really tired of hearing his numerous names and occupations. Sometimes he would be Jasvinder working at the KFC shop, on the other instances he would be Navjot assisting his Uncle in running his huge garment shop; although he never let the guys enter the shop saying that its very boring so let's go out.

Whenever he was asked about the yawning disparities between his Avatars and profiles, he would dismiss those thoughts simply with thunderous laughter and some cock and bull story.

"*Oye yaar*!! Everyone loves me so much out here that they have nicknamed me as per their affection for me. Some even think that I look like their daughter Kavleen so they have nicknamed me Jas - Leen. Now you only tell me what to do dear in this case??" And he would just hug them in his BIG arms against his bear chest.

The team neither believed nor distrusted him. There was no need to do either. He was a fun guy and the guys loved to be with him on the weekends apart from their other hangouts.

It was the day of the much awaited Quarter Finals of the World Cup between India and Pakistan. I bet that anyone who even knows how to spell the word "cricket" would do anything to watch this match. The guys were no exception and they were really restless like a software engineer waiting for his onsite opportunity, and amidst it, seeing instead his other colleagues being deputed every now and then.

The office work was somehow finished early and everyone left the office by 4:30. But it was yet a wild goose chase. The channels being broadcast by our cable guy did not have even a decent English channel; leave alone the possibility of the cricket match.

Standing at the bus stop, the guys looked as anxious as middle-aged aunties wearing make up more than their own body weights and fearing a huge thundershower from the skies.

Well, as always the team bumped into Jasbeer who was coming from the airport after his two week stay in Barcelona (The team had stopped believing his boasting overseas trip stories since once we saw him working at a local dockyard during his so called client meetings).

"Hey!! Left the office so soon guys?" He once again swung his big palms in the air to land a BIG smack on Hrishi's shoulders but he stepped back expecting the blow early and avoided it.

"*Oye*!! Tell me the matter guys ... you know I have a solution for all your problems."

"Whether or not they are not meant to solve our issues..." Krishna muttered, who had already started sulking after hearing that India was batting first.

"What ... what are you saying, Crushne?" He rolled up his sleeves; he never pronounced the name of Krishna correctly.

"Nothing ... nothing Jassi... We are feeling low and pissed off because we are not able to watch the Indo-Pak match..." Rajeev said.

"That's it?? You should have told me earlier man..." He gave us a look as if we were the lesser mortals having no right to live anymore...

We raised our heads in great hopes, just the way cricket players keep their heads up hoping for rain while losing a one day match.

"Let's move, we would go to Zaheer's shop." He declared and started moving without waiting for rest of the guys to follow.

The team was stuck at the bus stop, not sure whether to fall for the temptation.

The reason was obvious. Zaheer's Café was an infamous and a dark place and, based on the stories about this so called evil place, all that could be dreamt about was a gloomy and shady pub, crowded with cowboys and crooks puffing out cigar smoke and sharing sleazy jokes.

But eventually the charm of Sachin's straight drive and Pathan's Yorkers overshadowed the dread of the grimy stories and we started following Jassi like the little chickens after their mom.

Soon they entered that part of city, which they had never explored and little they knew about this dingy place. It was one of those areas where the sun never reaches. But all we could think of was the ticking of the score boards and not the yelling and fighting of the rogues fighting around the betting boards.

The moment we entered the café, the first thing that hit our senses was the pungent smell of beer and rotten fish fried in cheap oil.

"Did we take a shortcut to reach some Mumbai dance bar??" Hrishi cribbed and winked.

"Shut up idiot, don't you see what kind of awful ambience is this, let's get out of here," Krishna mumbled with tight lips.

Rajeev, on the other hand, was calmly scrutinizing every corner of the room till he set his hawk eyes on the small TV which was surrounded by hazy smoke and a bunch of yelling hooligans.

Slowly the team moved ahead, even though sniffing a small hint of danger. It seemed exactly the way a mouse steps forward into a trap, inevitably enticed by the juice of the hanging piece of the bread, in our case, it were the juicy strokes of our favourite players.

They shouldered their way amidst few questioning and staring eyes and let their bodies' slump into a resting position on unknown shoulders and backs.

After that day, it became a routine for the TEAM to go and have a fun time at the café. Krishna and Rajeev even started having few swigs of beer with few acquaintances they made there. But like Jassi, they also had changing names and careers and we blamed it all on the kicks from the big Patiala pegs they kept on having throughout the day.

It was one of those days when all of them were comfortably seated around a table, having big swigs from the beer mugs. It was the 2nd round match in Wimbledon where the new teen sensation from India, Anisa Zarin was playing…

The team was discussing the depths of her foreplay's hand … Oops … actually I meant the forehand's play. (Blame it on the Beer, chaps.)

Suddenly, Rajeev felt the thump of a burly hand on his shoulders.

Without turning back, he smiled and answered, "Hey Jassi… Whatzzzz up, so late today?" He mumbled and chewed the words in his mouth.

The answer he got was all Greek to him. Not because Jassi was too drunk and blabbering.

It was actually Greek, as the reply came from a Greek Police inspector, studded with his revolver and stars.

"Can I see your passports and work permits … of both … of you all?" Again, the uneven rubbles of English words fell from his mouth.

They all quickly frisked our pockets and the team cursed their luck in unison. They always carried their passports with them but they never had a tryst with the police on the tunnel kind of short cut that connected to this place and were least expecting one here.

"Actually we work in the Bank ... You know the Gamaporiki Bank, Sir!!" Hrishi tried to speak as softly as possible, realizing that it echoed back without making any impact.

The burning eyes were still glaring at us ... almost poking into our bodies. We looked around for "Jassi and gang" but they had vanished way before.

The team passed that weekend in police custody, and were charged with the grave crime of being a part of the gang which was involved in providing illegal entry into Greece to immigrants from all over India.

The rest was a nightmare; the issue was escalated to the SCT Trans Europe Relationship manager. Hrishi and Krishna were sent back to India and Rajeev had to bear the brunt of the whole incident as he was fired from SCT due to lack of abilities to manage the team; rather ending up in screwing it altogether.

Hrishi had to wait for another long six months before he could fetch himself a job in a call centre.

Krishna was rather lucky, due to his previous performances and client appreciations, he could make it again back to the same project. It took some time till he could make it back to Greece due to the not so generous remarks scribbled by the Greek authorities in his passport.

Jassi aka Jasbeer aka Jasvinder proved to be an illegal immigrant from Saudi Arabia involved in the illegal human trafficking across borders.

No one ever knew what went wrong with Rajeev.

It's been a real long time since this series of unfortunate events happened.

Wondering why I am telling all these things to you??

My full name is Raghav Krishna Acharya Shastri and that's why I would never let another ill-fated run of incidents again hit my TEAM in this unknown and foreign land!

Chapter 8: My Best Friend's Greek Setting

Greece, apart from the many incentives recounted by me, had another added bonus which no other US and UK onsite could offer and that is the fact that our languages are "Greek to each other."

My fun was limited to giving my expert's opinion with the liberty of uttering the most generous eruptions of emotions which used to come straight out of my heart at the very sight of the beauties walking past…

Mayank took a step forward and made better use of our rich cultural heritage.

It was another lazy Sunday afternoon when I was just stretching myself on the couch and doing the hopeless channel surfing since I knew that the meaningful ones would start later in the night.

Suddenly I saw Mayank coming out of the bathroom, with the hint of strong perfume on his body and a lot of glisten of the gel in his hair. He came and stood in his favourite akimbo style, facial expressions ready to reveal a lot but a posture to conceal it all.

"Hey May-Hunk ... Where to dude...?" I flattered him hard to get the most out of his system.

"Just make a wild guess ... The wildest of your dreams...," he said, tossing his hair back in style... He was giggling by now.

"Ok boss. So you are going on a date ... but with whom...?"

"The blonde beauty ... with big and big and very big ... eyes and very bouncy and wiggly ... hair..." He chuckled sheepishly.

"Kill the suspense dude ... tell me who is she?" I was getting more and more anxious...

"Cyn…Thia" He took extra long time to stretch the name at his will.

"What???" I was SHOCKED and that was an understatement ... you met this lass last week in the meeting and now you are out on a date ... that's an achievement.

Hats off to you!!"

But I was still not satisfied and desperately wanted to know more… How could you do it, man, and I was just working my ass off while he cracked the vital deal...

He could gauge my mind clearly as he flashed a wicked smile again and said "Wanna know how I did that?"

"Yeah ... tell me." I was almost running around like a dog now trying to look for his lost piece of bone.

"I have told her that I would teach her Indian Yoga and Indian languages on Acropolis Rock!!"

Acropolis Rock!! His intentions were clear... It was a famous hangout for the lovely and mushy couples half lying and sitting around in very cosy postures ... if you are venturing there alone then your experience would be greatly frustrating.

"Did she agree...? I mean, she is no idiot … not to understand your intentions..."

"Initially she doubted me but later on she agreed after I told her that it is the perfect peaceful heaven where the souls can get lost in the God almighty..."

"I know what it is that you want to get lost into??" I was getting exasperated now ... not on his achievement but at my inabilities.

"...." He was now laughing so much that he started rolling over on the sofa...

"But what do you know about Indian Yoga ... and what Indian languages do you know apart from Hindi and C++...?" I was really getting heated up and uttering any crap!

"What does she know about Yoga and Indian Languages ... Nothing ... whatever postures I explain to her as Yoga, she is bound to agree on that ... won't she?"

"Mayank this is not right dear..." I tried my level best to look honest but I was seriously thinking of ways to get the contacts of some other HOT chicks in the office.

"Okay! Mr Ethics Counsellor, You complete your guidelines on 'How NOT to have a girlfriends -- 100 ways' ... Allow me to go now."

And in a flash, he was gone ... humming some English track and whistling...

It was sheer boredom to stay alone home... I made some tea for myself ... then a sandwich ... and tried to lay my hands on some old English novels lying in the book shelf but nothing worked.

I finally did some workout just to tire myself to the brink and then I fell asleep.

It was a continued round of thumps on the main door that woke me up with a start. "Who is the idiot who doesn't even know where the call bell is?" I thought getting really annoyed.

When I peeped through the magic eye, I just could not believe my eyes... It was Mayank. The moment I unlocked the door he yanked it open and rushed directly inside as if an untamed circus lion had been set free in the jungle after ages...

I quickly traced the zigzag path he had followed to make a crash landing on the sofa ... he was coughing and humping over and over, and his chest was heaving like big amplitudes of sine waves.

"Hey Mayank, what happened bro... Are you ok?" I asked and handed him over the water bottle.

He was still struggling to regain his breath back as he gulped the water down his throat in one go... It took him another good five minutes before he uttered the first few words...

"You were right dude, I should not have done any such cheat-act on anyone ... God screwed me royally and beautifully." Apart from being on the verge of tears, he was looking a complete tragic hero.

I tried to control my outburst of laughter but after all my attempts it leaked past my lips and I flashed a wicked smile… Mayank nodded his head as if admitting his mistake.

"Tell me, what went wrong Mayank...," I tried my best not to sound patronizing though I desperately wanted to do so.

"Long story *yaar* ... I don't know how and where to start from…" He was gazing afar as if trying to look into a hazy picture and decipher it...

"Tell me how it all happened... I won't disclose it to anyone, man ... I promise," I said though I was all set to broadcast it to the entire world.

"Ok... Here is how it goes…" He took a deep breath as if to decide whether to disclose the humiliation story or not and then carried on...

"First I took her to the 'Athens Indo' Taverna (Similar to our Indian *dhabas* but you can't find any Sardar truck drivers there)." He said with an ironical smile as if the fond memories were about to get screwed up.

"WOW ... that was such a cool idea Mayank … The confluence of cross cultures ... you are very smart dear." First time I was praising his ideas because I knew they turned into a big-time fiasco.

He glared at me with his red eyes as if trying to say "Now you are having the real fun dude, eh?" On the surface, he carried on in his hushed and meek voice.

"Everything was going fine till the Indo-Pak love spoiled my love life to the hilt…" He leaned back on the sofa.

"What happened, the police asked for your passport thinking of you as some illegal immigrant…?" I was just imagining in what all possible ways he could have been humiliated.

"It was not Police or any other investigation ... I was getting real close with her and about to start with my 'Get-Close-Asana' ... and then…" He stopped in sheer silence as if something got stuck in his throat.

"...." The real part was yet to come!

"Along came a cross border friend all the way from Karachi or Dhaka ... I have no idea ... But he just came and started talking to me so amicably in Punjabi that I really didn't know what to do!!"

"But what's the problem dude...? What do you expect an Asian bro to do when he catches the sight of another ... that's understood *yaar*!"

"I have no objections with that at all man but the problem is that the guy was a flower seller ... you know ... clad in a typical hippie kind of dress and trying his best to understand how I grew from a flower seller to a person who could take a beautiful Greek Goddess out for a date."

"He thought you to be a flower seller…?" This time I couldn't help laughing out very loud!

"Yeah ... and when I whispered in his ear that I work in IT software industry, just to shoo him away, all he asked was, what kind of flower shop is that?" He slapped his forehead with his palm as if the whole disastrous scene got replayed in front of his eyes.

I was sitting down on the floor now, trying to control my laughter ... and Mayank was uttering some real good words for me.

"The last part of the story is real tragic, he halved the bunch of flowers he had in his hands and asked me to come along to sell the flowers together ... God damn it." He hid his face in his bent knees.

"...".I was getting back to my normal intermittent chuckles and giggles now.

"I almost had to jerk my hands away from his grip and I started running after Cynthia who was fuming by now, thinking that I actually do this job in my spare time…" He lifted his face up to let it rest on his forearms.

"So this is how it ended ... But this is not the end of the road ... there are other lasses around you can start with ... or you can even ask Cynthia to meet you, just to patch up again."

"You don't get it Raj, this is not the end of the story ... this is way too torn apart to have any kind of patch up dear…," he said in a hopeless tone.

"WHAT!!" What is still left...? That made me so happy with a rush of sadistic pleasure going down my heart ... oh I was right in being a defensive ostrich ... never poke your neck out way too much!!

"But what happened after that? Did she wait for you to come and talk to her ?" I was just praying hard that they did not have a patch up act there and then ... God save the Ostrich please!!

"I almost ran to catch up with her when she was about to get into her car ... and somehow explained that there was some BIG confusion which led to all that melodrama..."

I knew Cynthia had an Audi ... Mayank was really making me a big time jealous man.

"And she did agree to that ... I was so very much relieved man, she even held my hand then while we sauntered down to the Acro Rock."

I guess it was time for my Ostrich either to get buried alive or jump into the sea to end the shameful life.

"We went there and she rested her head on my shoulders while we enjoyed the sunset..."

The ostrich was sinking… F1 … F1 anybody?

"Our faces got real close ... as the sweet breeze of evening hit her cheeks ... a few strands of hair rolled over her forehead ... I just set them aside..."

Jealousy was a very small statement for my feelings ... I felt something burning ... my heart ... my soul … my *&!@!!!

I was surprised by the sudden long pause in the running commentary of Mayank's script... "C'mon, tell me that you kissed her, didn't you."

"I could have and I would have ... but what I got then was a tight slap that landed right on my cheeks...."

I was not able to make the connection... "But why would she hit you Mayank, it was a bliss of kiss from the miss." I happily sang my kindergarten rhyme.

"It wasn't she, idiot ... It was Athena who hit me..." He spread his hands out wide as if to make me understand the reality.

The ostrich was dead now ... I was dying for one ... he was doing a double cross!!!

"I took her out last week for the Yoga classes and told her that I won't be meeting this weekend since my mom is not well back home in India so I was not feeling like going out at all. She slapped me real hard and almost injected her pencil heels into my toes saying 'Is this the nurse who is making your mom heal sooner'?"

The ostrich had grabbed the life guard very hard now ... Sometimes the morals should not be inferred till the story is finished!!

"Tch ... Tch... that's sad baby ... better luck in next class ... This time you were made to do a 'Get-Slap-Yoga' only, eh?"

"What if I tell you that I was not done yet honey ... would you stop grinning? I know you are having loads of fun..." Mayank sprang up and kicked my ass real hard.

"WHAT ... what is still left there that you were not stripped off Manky...?" I was pulling his name's pronunciation closer to 'Monkey' since he was jumping like one.

"It was my Black Sunday, man ... both my birds have flown after scratching and beating me black and blue ... I hardly had a choice but to come back home and sleep peacefully in my cocoon."

"So, what went wrong, I hope they didn't hand you over to the cops?" I got a little worried now.

"No man, I met the super cop Raghav on my way back." His facial expression showed what emotions he had gone through.

"And then..." He kept on talking "Since we met real close to the office he dragged me to get the documentation done for last week's meeting." A real bad hair day for the man with so much of air.

"I am hungry man, the slaps and kicks have kicked my appetite... Can we cook something?" He got up with his palms over his aching butt and cheeks.

"That's what we are going to do... Let's move, we'd have our life saviour Maggie or *Khichdi* ... Let's move." I waved my hand at him.

We stood ... ready to strip down to our uniforms ... when Mayank turned and hugged me real close and tight.

I was so shocked at this sudden emotional outburst that I couldn't even wrap my hands around his back and they hung loose. To make the air a little less tense I just cracked a joke.

"So this double trouble made your orientation change drastically man?"

I could almost feel as if he was sobbing ... all I could hear in the feeble voice of his were the words ... "I miss you Ragi..."

"Ragina ... Ragilia ... Ragisha..." Another girlfriend ... another heartbreak ... you are one lucky bastard chap!!"

We were about to move to the kitchen when Nayana called up. As always, that made me smile so much that I almost blushed.

"One minute dude," I told Mayank and moved out of the house, avoiding his winks and whistles.

"Hi Raj, how was your day...? I got bored the entire day ... nothing to do on the weekend ... you didn't even come online."

I was about to tell her that even I had a very boring day. Then I thought of something, which was a strange blend of my frustration of the entire day and of the multitasking proficiencies of Mayank.

"Well Nayana, I went out on a date with a girl from my office, I went for a movie and coffee."

"Oh, that sounds amazing ... you are back so soon, should have spent some more time ... right?" She was definitely not very happy about what I just told her.

"O Nayana ... I was just..." She interrupted me in the middle so the "kidding" word could never come out of my mouth.

"Mom is calling ... will call you later..." She slammed down the handset to leave me alone with the beep-beep.

IT WAS NOT YOUR DAY RAJ. DON'T ACT SMART!!!

When I entered the flat, Mayank was giggling. He definitely had overheard my conversation.

"Shut up Monkey, come to the kitchen and let's make something…" I shouldered him away hastily.

We cooked our Maggie and that was the peaceful end of the night.

That was what I thought.

My sleep was broken by someone chatting right over my head ... I sat up in the night and saw it was 3:00 in the morning ... It was Mayank who was talking on his cell, hanging his torso halfway down from the balcony.

It took me some time to understand the words he was uttering and for my sleep to get demystified.

"See Maria, it's simple ... Just bend your head forward ... touch your right ankle with the left hand ... NO, No ... you are not getting it ... Should I come over next Friday night to explain it all to you??"

An Ostrich is one jerk of the highest order who is supposed to die after doing NOTHING in his life ... NOTHING is the word.

Chapter 9: Age of Vampires

"Lights, Camera and Action." This is how the 'takes' for our Hindi movies start…

Let me tell you the story of a different world the punch line for which is:

"Lights off … Web Cam … and Action all night."

I know this doesn't make much sense to you, but believe me it will when I lead you into it.

Before you start frowning and wondering what place and time I am talking about; let me tell you that all of us go through this phase in our lives at some point or the other.

Hi, I am Mayank Duggal and I am taking you four years back into memory lane, when I was in my final year of Mechanical Engineering.

I did my BE from an REC and for those who think that it stands for Regional Engineering College, let me tell you that it stands for "Resting in Eternal Comfort."

It might sound shocking, well, the toughest part of an REC is making it into it. After that life becomes quite easy. Semester after semester kept on passing by as coolly as the days of cricket test matches. Even if you can't level the score, batting through to the end would ensure a draw for you.

The only slight exception being the final semester egg-jams which feel like the real pressure and anxiety of the final slogging overs of a one-dayer.

This was the time when the dreams start to shape up; be it about our careers or the blooming of our sugar-coated mushy dreams.

Out of all the memorable things that happened at our hostel, the one that stood out was the advent of high speed internet that made its way when I was in the first year.

Life drastically changed because of this change, as it brought about a big globalization in the hostel life. The focus of the all the hunks drifted from the damsels of the college to Maries from France and Elizabeths from UK, courtesy a new Friendship site launched, named "CuteOrbit". This worldwide movement changed everything. A lot of inspired chatters started disappearing from the classes at odd times to catch up with their overseas girlfriends. For the rest, sleeping habits started matching with their South American nocturnal friends, namely. bats and owls.

Although, I was not fully influenced by this universal association, yet I could not keep myself away from all this for long and fell into one of the trajectories of CuteOrbit.

It was one of those cold nights of December when the hostel was looking like Dracula's mansion, studded with the random array of dark, pale and white windows. I entered my room after having a long GD (Gossip of drunkards, in case you thought it to be some serious group discussion). I got myself seated in front of my PC and entered the absorbing "calling hearts" chat environment.

I ceaselessly tried my hands on the butterflies and cute_angels; it was all in vain and I was about to log off, when there was a chat window that vibrated and pulsated on my screen like the throbbing of a heartbeat.

My heart definitely skipped one as I saw the charming name "Ragini_da_Mystery".

Ragini_da_Mystery: Hi I am Ragini, 23/f, I am a S/W engineer, nice chat name!!!!

I was too nervous even to reply to her message before she fired another hot message.

Ragini_da_Mystery: "Hey Dude....wanna talk dear??"

My immediate reaction was so overwhelming as if she had asked me out on a blind date.

Maverick _Hunk:"Hey yes!! Why not .....I am Mayank from ...'

It all felt like a reverie because along came her name, profession and contact details as well, though after some pleading but it was worth all the effort...

After two months of chatting and sugar-coated late night mushy talks, covered under the blanket and the quilt, we met on our first date.

She definitely was my dream-girl, tall, slender and having a dusky complexion. I saw her and fell in love. Only later on I got to know that she also fell head over heels the first time her eyes met mine.

Time flew too fast as the next thing I remembered was the day we got through our campus jobs and she got 'Bangalored' to Sifycon, a giant in the field of Finance Management.

I got placed in TesMac, it was my dream company as I was always a networking geek and wanted to work in the field of mobile technology solutions. But there was a glitch.

I got Gurgaoned!!

I did not give a thought before I gave up the idea of switching to my favourite company as the only thing I could plan and perceive at that moment was the comfort of being in her arms and getting myself lost in her eyes.

Bangalore is a paradise for the IT workers; if you can trade off a little on the package, you can get an IT job of your choice easily. Even if you frown a bit, you get to see the guys around doing honorary jobs and you start respecting every penny that your job would make you earn.

I made my way into a company called InfoSystems, which was not a giant like TesMac but I cared a damn as it was paying well and, apart from everything else, it gave me the golden perk of seeing my sweetheart at the end of every day, taking her care in the best possible ways.

Days, months and a complete year passed, and it all felt like one of those movies in which everything goes fine all the way and culminates in a perfect marriage.

But this didn't continue forever, and after the end of one long day I found myself arguing with my boss, with an envelope in my hand that had changed my world in a matter of just few moments.

It was my termination letter so lovingly called a pink slip.

"See Mayank, I can't help you dear," Chirag, my boss, didn't even bother to take his eyes off the monitor.

"But Sir, I have always delivered my level best and all the work has been appreciated by the client also." I was almost begging with my hands folded.

"It is not a question of your job only as it is a mass termination of the jobs due to the organizational restructuring on account of the business needs." His hands stopped on the keyboard for a few seconds; as a small gesture of sympathy for me.

For a moment, I felt as if I was a street dog, given the explanation that his killing is a part of the mass cull done by municipality and so he should not feel bad about it.

He carried on, "See Mayank, the company had an expansion plan in India that didn't go the way they wished so they are just cutting short on their operations."

It was useless talking to him, little he could do about it. So I just completed my separation formalities and walked off.

I met Ragi in the evening and told her about everything.

"How would I take care of you now honey?" I was about to rest my head on her shoulder when she stood up in a flash.

"Mayank, actually I was about to tell you that I am going to UK for a year." I felt a surge of dryness in her tone but I blamed it all on my gloomy mindset.

"That's great Ragi, at least we can have enough to start our new life and meanwhile I would get a decent job as..."

"Mayank, we cannot carry on like this anymore... I think we should part ways now." The dryness in her voice was not my illusion for sure.

The words fell into my ears like molten glass. What does she mean by "Not Working???"

"Ragini, but is love not the name of sacrifice, didn't I leave my dream job for you and was I not here just for you?" I never wanted to say those words but I had no choice.

"If you have no sense of maturity about your life and career, don't expect me to follow suit blindly sweetheart."

."But didn't I take care of you in every moment...?" I was almost choking at seeing this new face of my sweetheart.

"That is the whole problem Mayank ... You made me a bloody bloodsucking leech. A parasite who is dependent on you, for all my needs. I can't live with a man who is nothing but a love sick dude, has no job, and has no standing of his own."

"I always wanted to be around you ... since you needed me ... I love you Ragi." I just wanted to cry my heart out to her.

"You never loved me ... had you done that you would have tried to groom an individual out of me."

I was never too good in mastering the art of playing around with words and she was just spinning a beautiful yarn of them around me. I could see that she was willing to walk out; that too after putting the blame on my head.

"Good bye Mayank, I am sorry that we spoiled a golden year of our lives, but I wish you all the best for your future."

She turned away and she didn't even turn her head.

I came back home and I don't know for how many hours I was sitting in the darkness, not knowing what to do.

I had only seen it in the movies where the negativity strikes someone so heavily that all he can think of is depressing thoughts and their severely damaging consequences. I was sitting on the edge of my bed, forehead supported by my fist.

God! Would you send someone from the heavens for my exorcism from these disgusting thoughts?

I tried to shrug off the pestering thoughts but they were like bugging chain mails with silly attachments. Even if you try to shrug them off by just forwarding them to the next victim, they would come again with a bigger baggage to nag you. I just couldn't understand what to do in this situation...

But what put an end to all my hopes of life was the way Ragi walked away from me.

It was impossible for me to live without her. Every moment of our (or I should say 'My' now) lives were inseparable from each other. Starting from the pleasant "Good Morning" that used to shove life into us for the whole day to the mesmerizing "Good Night" that led us into the dreamy world. Not a single breath I took without thinking about her. I could not imagine of having anything since all I could think of were her tender and soft fingers feeding me the first bite without having sipped even a drop of water.

God!! How can you do this to me? If she had to go away from me then why did you make us love each other so much the in first place?

I had heard this famous dialogue: "You always have a choice that you can make in your life." Indeed I had, either to carry the burden of my own corpse on my shoulders or to put an end to it right here and right now.

"End"!! "I am going to end my life this way?"

Death always scared me a lot. What scared me the most about ending life was the question "IS there life AFTER death?" But my life had become so hopeless and so sickening that I asked myself "Is there life BEFORE death. Am I living or I have just become a vegetable??"

All of a sudden death seemed like a soothing embrace which would absorb all my pains and put me to a soothing sleep.

I walked down to the room and latched the door back. The pitch darkness again surrounded me and I just felt the strong urge to get enveloped into this gloominess. The very idea of all the sufferings coming to an end made me feel so relieved. I sat on the cold floor, my head buried in my bent knees, and I didn't know when I started sobbing.

"No Mayank," a voice came from within me... "You can't do it. There should be a way out."

"Ok! So be it, tell me what COULD be the way out??" my tussle with my own heart and mind started.

"What about your parents ... how would they feel to see you shattered and broken like this?" The mind tried to drift my thoughts to the responsibilities I should be shouldering for my parents.

"Seeing me breaking and my life being in shambles every day, let them face the reality today." I was firm on my negative stand.

"What about your career Mayank, I know it's not rocking as of now, but it's not on a bottom low as well."

"Ragini was the centre of all my ambitions and my hard work. Who should I trust now? This all feels like a mirage now. Nothing is real." I walked up to the centre of the room and stood on the chair.

Today what feels so scary and akin to a fanatical thought to me, it then felt like the only way out of my miseries. Standing on a chair and slowly forming a rope out of the bed sheet...

It was then that my phone rang.

I didn't care to see who it was as it mattered least to me now.

What mattered was the fact that I had set a previous recording from Ragini as my ring tone.

"Mayank ... Mayank ... Mayank ... I love you my Hunk ... never ever leave me."

"Only if you cared to stay with me." My tears had dried up as I tied the rope to the fan.

"If you try to leave, I would hug and wrap my arms around you...," I could actually imagine her cheeks going pink when she said so.

I silently wrapped the sheet around my neck. The prisoner of life was about to be set free from earthly bonds.

"The touch of your hands says you'll catch me, wherever I fall..."

I could not take it anymore, my throat felt choked with overpowering emotions and that was it... In the spur of the moment I kicked the chair ... with my toes.

A sharp sting in my neck and I felt as if I was falling down from the peak of a cliff ... then it was all dark and very cold around me...

If you ever had the ill fate of getting drowned and then someone rescued you after some moments, you would actually know how it feels like to experience the huge gush of air, when it hits the much deprived lungs of your body.

I regained my consciousness with a start; coughing ceaselessly for more air and I yanked opened the window. My knees had given way to take my body weight so I had just slumped down onto the floor.

My phone was thrown in a corner, the recording was about to finish and Ragini was still humming the last lines of the song.

So I was alive!! But how did I survive. I couldn't remember even a fraction of what happened after I kicked the chair but there was nothing that I could recollect apart from a sinking feeling getting over me.

Bit by bit the skewed memories got linked together and I could actually see the rushes of my *kamikaze* act with my blood red eyes.

My knot with death was not destined now as the knot I had wrapped around my neck gave way too soon and gave me one more chance to live.

I took the call, it was from a local landline number.

"Who is this??" My throat pained like hell as I ran my fingers on the red welts on my neck.

"Is it Mr Mayank I am talking to?"

"Yes...," I kept the expenditure of words to the minimum.

"Actually I am Deepak calling from a job counselling team, Job Shifters and I got your resume from MobJob.com and I want to..."

I was listening to all he was saying, but paying little attention. Was this a hint from somewhere that it was not over now? I had to live ... rather than end it for someone so ruthless who never cared for me.

Is this call an indication for me that one lost opportunity opens the gates to thousand other ones ... be it for a job or any bitch that ditches you.

I would live and live it only for me ... I would become self-centred to the hilt even if makes an eccentric selfish bastard out of me.

And I would take every Ragini in this world to task ... I would teach her what it means to play with someone's emotions and sentiments.

"Hello ... hello ... Mayank are you there...?" Deepak was shouting at the other end.

"Yes Deepak, I am very much interested in the job profile that you just described ... tell me is it going to be a telephonic or face to face..."

And this is how I made it to SCT and came to Greece ... since then I have left no stones unturned to make it a permanent stay at the onsite.

This is Mayank four years after that shock, and I am very happy with the way I am doing today.

On the surface I show that I love and care for everyone around me. But Raj is my favourite as he is a "Ridiculously Adorable Jerk!!" He does not know his worth. Despite having brains and all the capabilities, he never tries to realize his own potential.

All he can do, throughout the day is to chat and play chain mails with his girlfriends. I know he is doing very well with the QPM initiative but I need this thing at any cost.

I want to reach to the top and I have to walk over a few bodies. I want more of Rajs in my team, because when I walk over him, he still keeps on smiling; basking in the glory of thoughts that he is bridging a small gap for me.

Chapter 10: The Other Side of the Fable

After the boring experience of the last few Sundays, I decided to do anything but stay home. I was bored of the beaches after the initial excitement of seeing the benefits of sunbathing.

It was too early for the pubs and bars so even that was not an option.

The only place that was left where I could go was my office, check my mails and browse some of the 'Favourite' marked sites.

After Mayank left for his weekly Yoga tutorials, I also had my breakfast and left for office.

It took me only an hour to revisit the favourite sites and check my mails and forwards. I got restless again and started tapping my fingers on the keyboard, not knowing what to do.

I arched my back, staring at the roof, thinking hard to decide how to kill the next few hours.

Suddenly something struck my mind, not really something important but something that would help me to kill some time at least.

I remembered that while giving me the handover, Sundeep had told me that he was working on the same PC that was given to me.

"So please clean those mails when you get time. There are some important and related stuff to QPM as well which are of no use to me, so make the most of them."

I remembered his instructions and his selfless smile.

Well!! I have all the time in the world for it today, thank you God.

And what better way than to read all of them, I know they would be boring, but I had no better options.

I started scanning mails one after another; minutes of meetings, project documents and boring officious commanding mails from Rampaging Raghav.

My scrolling eyes got hooked on to a month old mail from Sandy that was written to Raghav. It was the subject line of the mail that caught my attention as it read in caps: "QPM: THE FINAL PROPOSAL PRESENTATION".

Sandy was never a part of QPM. Then why the hell was he sending the final presentation to Raghav and that too a month before we started the meetings for QPM?

I was clueless and so I started reading the contents of the mail:

"Hi Raghav,

Since my machine is having some problems with the mail set-up, sending you the presentation from Sundeep's ID.

Please review it and revert back to me if further changes are required.

Thanks and Regards,

Mayank"

"MAYANK!!!" I felt as if I just fell from the skies. You are a cheap bastard and you have no right to write "Regards" as you have no regard for ethics and morals of the corporate world. I cursed and sulked thinking about how he always fooled around and acted as if he was the last person on this earth who was serious about the whole proposal.

I was here to kill the time and now this bad time was killing me.

I clutched my hair in frustration ... QPM was my dream and I worked so hard for it … to see it grow from scratch … like a toddler is watched curiously by its parents from the moment when it starts walking on its own.

Sundeep, why are you such a dodo? Why you never doubt others? It should have been the most critical part of your handover, why can't you be a little more shrewd?

"Did he say something about this during the handover?" I asked myself. But I didn't listen even to a minute of it. I was actually finding it hard to keep my eyes open and so I had recorded the entire conversation on my mobile.

"What is the very point of even playing it now? Mayank has already taken the credit for QPM." I felt my heart sinking.

"What is the harm in listening to it? Maybe Raghav had not liked his proposal at all." I tried to think in the right direction and left my seat to pace up and down the room. I always believed that it helps release the stress.

I opened the recording folder and started paying attention to something I was supposed to do two months ago. Better late than never.

I played, paused and replayed forty minutes of the intensive session. It had process flow, frequent client queries and even few comments on my careless attitude.

But it had NOTHING about QPM.

The only thing that was related, were the repeated instructions to clean up his mails from my machine.

I didn't want to leave any checkbox unchecked, so I quickly dialled Sandy's number.

"C'mon, pick it up....!" I gritted my teeth hard as the devotional caller tune on his cell played repeatedly.

A drowsy voice greeted me from the other end. "Hey Raj, what's up dude, I hope you are not working on Sunday *yaar* …"

I was feeling so sick that I was not in the mood of working even on weekdays. I somehow managed a reply. "Actually I am, Sandy. I have some doubt, so called you up!"

I quickly planted a question and put it forth. As usual, it was on his fingertips and he replied even before I finished.

"Actually Sandy, I was just cleaning up your mails from my system and deleted few mails without even reading them, so ..." I didn't want to utter the word "QPM".

"Don't worry. it was a mess and nothing important ... anyways, what were the subjects of those mails? Anything important?"

"Actually these mails were not sent by you... Mayank sent them." I cleared my throat in an attempt to sound casual.

There was a pause at the other end, as if he was trying to digest what I was saying.

My heart was beating very fast, say something about QPM man, Anything!!!

"Oh Mayank, yeah I remember that his mail was not working for sometime so he used my machine instead." Sandy finally broke the silence, not quite the way I wanted it to be.

"Shit!!" Sandy was the last hope I was banking on and he too couldn't do much about the whole mess. Mayank was too smart to leave a single trace.

He had even deleted the attachment from the sent mail.

"Then why the hell did he let the mail stay in Sundeep's PC?" I slumped back into my chair the moment I thought about this and cupped my forehead in my palm.

"Because Sandy is toothless, Raghav is always happy with his tail wagging and there was a buffer time of two months before I was yet to make an entry here."

"Hats off boss. You are a perfect bloody swine. I cannot get at par with you, never ever in my life."

For a moment, I thought of calling Mayank and giving him a good jab for his backstab. But that would not help.

"Raj, are you there ... Hello!!! ... Hello!!!..." Sandy was almost screaming from the other end.

His voice slowly died on me as I gently put the handset back to disconnect the call, my throat was way too choked to utter even a single word.

I was better off amidst the sugar-coated lies rather than getting goaded mercilessly into the bare realities of the real world.

The phone rang and I picked it up.

"Raj, are you doing ok dude? I feel something is definitely wrong dear." It was the soothing voice of Sandy.

"You are too late in realizing that Sandy!!" I decided to take at least one person, whom I liked so much, into confidence.

I told him everything. I had to cry my heart out to someone.

There was a hush at the both ends for next few seconds ... he was shocked and I was mocked.

"Raj, it's all because of me. I should have been a little more careful about what was happening at my system." Sandy was obviously shaken.

"Sandy, bygone is bygone ... It is Mayank's shrewdness, don't take the blame on you."

"But how could he do this? I mean the proposal was still in the pipeline, how could he get all the required templates and other reference documents from Raghav's machine?"

I knew it ... it was through the mischievous keystrokes stealer freeware program, courtesy Mayank.

"What are you thinking Raj?".in came the concerned voice of Sandy from the other end.

"It's a jungle out here Sandy, you were right ... I even doubt whether my presentation is safe here or not ... please help me out, man" I was everything but sobbing.

"Relax ... Raj, let me think ... Is your presentation complete now?"

"Almost ... 90 %, some finishing touches are to be given... But I am scared. What if he has already stolen it?"

"You do one thing Raj. You send that presentation to me. ASAP..."

What is he talking about, why does he need it now?

He continued, "Before you start doubting me as well, let me tell you that it would be a proof in written with me that, as of this date, you are the owner of this document."

"How would that help Sandy, if he has already stolen it?" I was way too depressed to act on this copyright plan.

"What if he has not done it yet Raj? Sometimes overconfidence renders you a lazy ass … and you are not loosing anything, right?" Sandy assured me with his calming words.

"Ok Sandy, thanks a lot for standing by me and helping me out." I felt as if I had rested my aching head on his shoulder.

"What else are friends for? And don't send it in a mail. Keep it on our shared location.

I will take it from there. Don't leave any trace. Trust me, your hard work won't be ruined."

"Thanks a bunch Sandy… I don't know how I…" I was really grateful to him.

"Shut up, cut the crap and hang up the call now… some freeware program might be listening to our conversation!!"

We chuckled as he made me smile and relaxed eventually.

Chapter 11: Of Rajmah, Marriages and Mirages

As the days of my return to India approached; Raghav undertook the ritual which is performed for everyone leaving for the homeland. You come here with lots of dreams, aspirations, and Indian sweets and go back with a blend of memories, all kinds of experiences, and foreign chocolates and liquors.

Anyways, it was a Thursday night when Mayank and I headed for Ravishing Raghav's place. Despite my requests, he took full two pegs of scotch before leaving.

I really got annoyed and told him tersely, "What is this Mayank...? You know that he has cooked *rajmah* and rice especially for us and this is how you are ready for the feast?"

Controlling all his body parts, which were swinging in all possible directions, he said, "*Yaar*! You are going to eat *rajmah* at an *Idli sambar* stall... You know what you'll get? Delicacies served in coconut oil." He chuckled sheepishly.

"This is not fair ... now why is it about he being from Kerala and we from Delhi?" I really didn't like the discrimination he was so fond of making.

We entered Raghav's place and were greeted by his 5 years old son, Omkar. We had already abbreviated the name as "OMKAR = One More Kamina and Additional Raghav," but he was really very cute, not at all like his father.

Raghav's wife was already frowning and making faces due to the musky gushes of the Black Label coming from the bay of Mayank's mouth. It took us some time to make her believe that it was the new and strong deodorant that Mayank had bought only last week. She was not convinced though as we could clearly gauge from her facial expressions.

"At least it smells better than what she has poured on her head..." Mayank whispered into my ears ... without realizing that he was whispering too loudly...!!

I kicked his ankles hard with my shoes and he screamed in pain.

"Hey Mayank, what happened … are you ok, man?".Raghav asked as we could see that he was really concerned.

"Nothing Raghav, I just hit the leg of the table…," he cursed me, gritting his teeth.

The dinner was good... I kept looking at the sulking Mayank after each bite that was going down. After the dinner, I whispered in his ear, "I wonder where all the coconut oil has gone, just feel your tummy; oops it's all in there!!"

Mayank would have hit me hard had we not been at Raghav's place.

After the dinner, we made ourselves comfy on the sofas and took sips from the filter coffee. Then came an unexpected blow at me from Mayank space centre.

"You know Raghav, Raj is going to get married to the girl of his dreams very soon." He said trying to locate the table and put the coffee back on it.

Now what is that Mayank, I know you have heard me talking to Nayana and observed me writing real long mails to her, but this is way too much dear, you just can't do that.

"Hey congrats Raj!! Who is she, someone from our company or some Greek goddess from the Bank?" Raghav asked, lifting Omkar in his lap who was now almost hanging from his moustache.

"Nothing Raghav ... nothing like it... He is just kidding." I tried to defend my fort.

"Ok, then tell Raghav why do you write waaaaay too long mails to someone special?" Mayank crossed his legs and winked hard at me and Raghav.

He had crossed the line, now he was trying to show that during office hours I do all this stuff. Where exactly are you taking it to Mr, that too in front of Raghav?

There was hush in the room for some time. I just hoped that Raghav did not take it way too seriously. He didn't supposedly because he broke the silence after some time.

"There is nothing bad in that Mayank... He is actually laying the foundation of a good life that is coming up his way... .After all, this is what love marriages are all about."

"So you are in favour of love marriage, Raghav?" Mayank turned towards Raghav now, leaving me rather relaxed in my chair.

Raghav picked up his head, as if measuring whether he was away from the earshot of his wife. Then he resumed confidently, "Oh yes, I strongly favour them guys..."

"What do you favour Raghu?" his wife got back from the kitchen, carrying banana chips in the tray.

We all could observe the flushed colour of Raghav's face and it definitely was not because of the little devil clutching his hair.

"Raghav was saying that he is in favour of having coffee right after the dinner for better digestion..." I admired myself for handling the situation beautifully.

"No Sudha, we were discussing the pros and cons of the different kinds of marriages and I said that I favour love marriage." Raghav took a big swig and flashed a big smile back to us.

"After all, ours had been a love marriage only…," she said with a big smile and sat next to Raghav, nudging him softly.

"WHAT"!!! That was the verbal translation of the emotions that we went through at that moment of time... Raghav couldn't get married this way ... The man who always gave priority to work...

The man who seemed to be in a nuptial knot with SCT rather than his personal life...

HE CAN'T DO A LOVE MARRIAGE!!

"I can read your thoughts guy ... but this is where we make the mistake to understand love."

Love…

OH!! So Mr Rollicking Raghav is going to explain the "requirements and architecture of love" to us ... go on man!! I was sure Mayank must be thinking the same even in his drowsy senses.

"We all think of love as only passion, being close to each other, staying happy, and life being a roller coaster ride ever after."

"That's what love is all about Raghav..." I expressed my deep understanding of love which was extracted from the overnight chat sessions and mushy late night talks over the phone calls.

"No dear, Love is all about responsibility. It's about the fact that even after staying miles away from each other for generations, the love does not fade away. Its about the trust that lays the foundation of the family and kids that you are going to have."

Mayank and I sat back in silence. We stared at Raghav with a constant gaze as if we were the hungry chimps, looking at their human counter parts in a zoo and waiting for their peanuts.

But what Raghav was saying was not at all peanuts. It made a lot of sense and we still could not believe that these were the words coming from his mouth.

"Love is all about making the other one feel that he or she is always there for the other one ... feeling the pain and happiness together and knowing what the other one is going through, without having to say even a single word."

I nodded in agreement ... what is the point of staying together in one house like strangers.

"What happened, Mayank? Sound like a boring lecture from your college professor?" Raghav joked. Mayank was sitting with eyes half closed and I knew that a single cup of coffee couldn't make up for 4 BIG pegs of Black Label.

"No Raghav ... I don't agree with you... What if the trust and faith is one-sided? What if you wait for all those years and she snaps it off by saying that it's not working?"

I never could believe that Mayank could have such bitter feelings towards love.

His monologue continued…

"What if she just says that you are not the man I loved 4 years back... What would you do and how would you react?"

"Mayank I would try to give her more of my time…," Raghav tried to pacify him.

"Time? It's all about how affluent or stable you are... Theoretically not in your classroom lecture but surely in our lives ... hiccc!!!"

I passed on a glass of water, but he raised his palm gesturing, "I am fine."

But he was not, he was very disturbed and it was not the scotch that was talking.

"The moment your life gets unstable, she starts sending signals that things are not working ... Just observe those signals!

If you can put the things back on track, she would just hug you saying you are my hero...." He paused for a moment, smiling as if recalling that moment.

Sadness ... Hatred ... vengeance. His face was portraying all the emotions in one moment.

"But if it is shattered..." The anguish again enveloped his face. "she would simply walk off ... saying 'I warned you earlier dude ... mend your ways else we part ways'

How cool is that??... Where should I fit it in your story ... Huh??"

The room was in hush now. Mayank looked like a Madame Tussauds' statue since even his eyes were not moving. But the tongue had done its job ... and the sting was real deep.

My heart went out to Raghav ... whatever he said made a lot of sense and was true ... But instead of getting a round of applause and clap, he was greeted by one tight slap.

Sudha broke the ice; she disappeared in the kitchen and came back with a pack in her hand. Just to lighten the air she said...

"See the supermarket guys are such idiots, I asked them for olive oil and they gave me grape wine instead ... Now this is what I call 'Lost in Translation' ... I'll have to throw it anyway."

Everyone tried to force a smile. I guess Mayank also realized that he had done something wrong so he just sprang up from his grave in the couch and said "Hang on, allow me. I'll throw it in the trash" and he dashed out in a flash.

I felt a lot easier and relaxed now... I glanced at Raghav and said."Whatever you said was right Raghav... Maybe Mayank has a different thought process."

Raghav nodded his head and said, "No Raj, I think I was lucky to have the right girl in my life... You become what life makes you think and what it takes you through."

We again slumped back into silence, sipping our coffees. Sudha again stood up after some time… "Care for another round of coffee, guys?? Where is Mayank?"

"Yeah sure!!" I said happily ... realizing that it was indeed too late ... So I just yelled "Mayank…" turning my face towards the balcony where he had disappeared.

"Take the devil's name and Mayank is here..." He indeed looked like one, with his hair in a mess and the blood red eyes!!

"Don't give me that look guys ... I was just catching up on some fresh air out there." He shrugged his shoulders as if shunning our questioning eyes.

I was sure it must have been the sight of some Greek beauty down the street or in the opposite house that he was catching up with.

As the Dracula slumped back into his grave again, I changed the topic with the most stale and common fashion. "So how is the weather going to be there back in India, guys?"

"Its going to be sweet and salty as such are the memories you will be carrying back with you, buddy." He said with difficulty as he had started having hiccups.

Mrs Raghav got back from the kitchen with coffee mugs – And seemed terribly concerned with the state of Mayank.

"Are you ok Mayank? Have some water ... here." She had to actually point at the water glass to make him understand where it was.

As I bent down close to him, to pass the tumbler to the lazy ass, I again felt a deep gush of 'aroma' from his mouth... I was not surprised by its presence but by the fact that it smelled completely different.

"What is it Mayank?? Did you take some more shots on the way?? But When??" I whispered in his ears, pretending to hand over the water to him.

Mayank did not move even an inch from his thoughtful posture and said the golden words:

"Whoever said that booze is the daughter of grape is my best man, dude."

I frowned furrowing my eyebrows in an attempt to make the connection ... but when I did ... It was very tough for me to keep my voice down.

"WHAT!! You gulped down half litre of grape wine?? Are you sick man??" I was really irritated now, yet concerned for him.

Mayank was laughing now; blabbering and mumbling the half chewed and half spit words... "Life is a bitch and so are girls... So girls are my life ... hicccc!!!!"

Raghav and Sudha were really worried now as Raghav asked me, "Is he ok Raj? There is a doctor down the street, should I call him, and he would be here in no time!" He sprang into action.

"No, Raghav ... ugh ... I think he is too drowsy ... couldn't sleep well last night."

Well that wasn't a complete lie... He really was engaged in his yoga classes way too late.

Saying that, I literally lifted him in my arms and whispered in his ears... "Mayank, please watch yourself... See where we are and what are we doing."

But Mayank was in some other world ... he was still on with his love sick tale ... "Why did you leave me...?"

You would get two birds for the one that you lost last weekend buddy ... but for now; please move. I dragged the booze tanker to the door.

His tongue was still not coming to peace like the rest of his body.

"You are right Raghav, love is strange, sometimes, you need to do what you are told not to and sometimes you needn't what you are told to ... very complex." Now that was irritating me ... or, I think, everyone by now.

Despite that, Raghav walked all the way to the lift, to see us off.

Only if the drunkard could curb his medley now... The latest that was shot off from his mouth was ... "Raghav, Raj likes *rajmah* because it sounds like 'Raj-Ma' ... reminding him of his mom ... funny isn't it?"

"Take care Mayank... Good night Raj...!" were the last words from Raghav that disappeared in air when the elevator door closed between us. I actually felt like being a body crutch for him.

It took a few gushes of chilled air and some caustic remarks from me to make him start rolling on his feet at least.

As we entered the corner of our street, I was feeling very lonely all of a sudden... What have I done so far apart from casually chatting with the girls for hours, knowing that it is all virtual and immature?

And here is this very different and mysterious girl in my life...

Is she in love with me, or I am in love with her??? But how much do I know her or understand love... All I know is that if I don't see her name in my inbox, I feel incomplete and irked ... that's it. What should I call it??

I was getting puzzled as we entered our flat and the cell rang. Mayank's crawling body came back to life for a split second thinking some of his Yoga aspirants called.

The moment he realized it was mine, he disappeared in his room...

It was not Raghav... It was a call from India made through a calling card... Why mom?? Why are you up so late ... don't spoil your health like this.

Shooting darts of a few more pungent remarks in Mayank's back, I picked up the call...

It was Nayana!!!

I felt as if my heart started beating again.

"Raj...," came the deep and longing voice, "I was feeling very lonely and don't know why I felt that you might also be feeling left out. Sorry if I bugged you dear!"

"No dear ... that's ok." I suddenly remembered Raghav's words.

"Love is all about making the other one feel that he or she is always there for the other one ... feeling the pain and happiness together and knowing what the other one is going through, without having to say even a single word."

I looked up to heavens and smiled, sending my thanks to the Almighty.

We talked for an hour that day ... and when we wished a sweet night to each other, with the plans and promises to see each other once I land in India on Saturday night.

I actually smiled for the first time in the day even when I had to pack for around next four hours to get my globally scattered clothes and other stuff into my suitcase and I didn't remember when I peacefully dozed off to sleep while doing that.

Chapter 12: Home Sweet Home

Well, phew!! I picked up my bag and moved to check whether the boarding had started, I stood up and started walking down. On airport you see all kinds of creatures (Well, Do not start looking for aliens)!! You see guys who come here for the first (and may be last) time. They are kind of amazed by the glitters of the tinsel town. They stand in every possible queue as they don't know where they need to go and they are too shy to ask anyone as well.

I am an annual member of the airport; because I pay a visit to this place once a year. I roam around like a tiger showing his prowess in his own wild terrain. Casting a glance at every possible place and giving everyone a very patronizing look. Until and unless we realize the fact that this is going to be over soon and the second chance would take another good year, the "take the world in your stride" attitude doesn't go away easily.

"Home Sweet Home" is the thing that hits the shores of our hearts and minds when we pack our bags to come back to India. The flag of India seems to be the only thing that makes us proud... The smell of "*Chola-Bhature*" and "*Rajmah-Chawal*" used to be the only thing that could make our nostrils flutter. Mom's love and the homely delicacies used to be additional bonus and pull.

I took one day off from the office to select the chocolates for the office, the best ones were obviously meant for Nayana, carefully selected and sorted. I bought the much asked for "Chivas Regal"; which was my pre-requisite entry ticket to the office, as specified by the friends out there.

Once again I started showing the traits of an annual member by pacing around here and there. But the blondes and redheads who used to attract my attentions and stole my breaths were looking dead boring now. I desperately wanted to get out of this place.

Once I entered the connecting flight to Delhi, I felt as If I had entered a "mini India". I saw an aunty who was comfortably seated by folding her legs above the seat, munching on her favourite snacks which she asked from the not-so-willing airhostess. If that was not sufficient, I saw a cosy honeymoon couple lost in their warm talks. But the cherry on the cake was stolen by a bunch of "turbanators" who kept on arguing with the crew as to why they couldn't be given more than 3 mini scotch bottles.

I got an aisle seat and I was very happy with it as it helps you in the extreme situations to cope with the forces of nature.

There was a lady sitting next to me, clad in a business suit. She was of my age only, maybe younger, but the seriousness worn along with the oval spectacles, clearly told that she was some big tycoon who only dealt with presentations and big board room meetings.

I greeted her… "Hi, how are you doing?" I just said that seeing a familiar Indian face in my row.

"Hi." She raised her head from her laptop and the reply was so crisp and dry that it simply drew a firewall of "Do not disturb" between us.

"Actually I am...," I started mumbling something and then gulped down my words in my throat. No use.

I just picked up one of those boring flight magazines which are studded more with ads and boring articles on culture and rituals.

The phone rang... Fortunately I had put the phone on the vibrator mode else the airhostess would have given me a glare as the plane was about to take off.

"Hey Mayank... Yea ... I am fine dear ... How are you doing dude...? Yeah I am also doing great ... Sure ... will do that ... *chal* take care and see you back soon."

Mayank was almost shouting at the other end and I had to literally keep the phone away from my ears to avoid the shrillness.

"Hi, I am Shweta Chopra, nice to meet you."

First I could not believe that the lady with the dry and crisp tone had extended her beautiful hand that was studded with diamond rings. She was actually smiling at me.

"Nice to meet you ... Shweta," I was still hurt with her first reaction.

"So you are going back to India ... from SCT?" She asked in a very soft tone, tucking her sleek laptop back into the case.

"Yea ... How do you know about that...?" I asked, crossing my arms over my chest ... Is she someone from a secret agency trying to steal the proposal. C'mon Raj, you are thinking too much.

"Just a wild guess, there are so many SCT guys flying to US and UK that it's always a safe guess to make." She arched back and tied her hair into a pony tail.

She was wearing a very expensive Hugo Boss perfume in addition to the affluent attire. There was something uncanny about this girl that I couldn't fathom.

I tried to stay relaxed.

"So how is your Gamaporiki Bank doing?" Her voice was husky and quite mysterious now.

What!!! She knows about our bank, who is she, someone from the hostile company trying to win over the bid from SCT. But why would they take so much of pain in this strange way?

"…" I stared back with a blank look.

"And how is Mayank doing Raj??" She uttered in a very cold voice that sent a chill down my spine. My thought process was completely sent into a whirlpool by the lady who was staring somewhere in the far, as if trying to identify the looming images of a mirage.

Shit!!! That was easy man and I was pulling it really way too far. C'mon Raj, Didn't you say "Hello Mayank" on the call. This is too much of your inquisitive thinking.

"Yeah, he is fine, doing well. But how do you know him, Shweta?"

She exhaled a big sigh as if there was a big storm going on inside her heart and she was just trying to vent it out.

"Because … my name is not Shweta … I am Ragini … Well it could well have been Ragini Duggal today … But see what I have made of myself now."

There was a sob and then an outburst of overflowing emotions that found their way out in form of tears and cries.

It took me some time to make the connection … Ragini Duggal … Duggal is Mayank's surname. Is she the ex-wife of Mayank…?

But Mayank never got married … WHO IS SHE…? I just shook my head in trying to set up the link.

Few heads turned from the adjacent seats and scanned me from head to toe as if I was the culprit who just made the beautiful lady wail.

"What is this all about Shweta … I mean Ragini?" I fidgeted in my seat and turned towards her. Getting ready to read through the story that was about to unfold.

After returning to a state of normalcy, she quickly ran through her fairy-tale of the rollercoaster ride that started with the man of her dreams, Mayank, and how it all got shattered; or rather how she made it end.

To be frank, I was quite fuming at her very selfish and materialistic attitude and had no sympathy at the very way she dumped Mayank.

"Don't you think you just chucked him out after using him?" "You bitch" were the last two words that I muttered too slowly to allow her the opportunity to hear.

"I know I did a perfectly bitchy act Raj. I hail from a rich business family and it was just helplessly in my system to use and throw things.

Even human beings were just merely either business networking nodes or exploitable items; take the juice in, throw the peel away."

If I had the powers of a wish master, I would have thrown her into the turbine blades of the plane and would have asked "How about your juices being squeezed out this way honey?"

"So you must be very happy now Ms Chopra, or is it Mrs Chopra??" I made my best effort to sound as insulting as I could.

She stayed hushed for few seconds and then resumed "Raj, once someone told me that heaven and hell are right here on this earth and you get back what you give to others."

"I don't believe it, what is it that you don't have today to come up with this philosophical quote…?" My fists were still clenched to smash her face into mashed potatoes.

"I don't have any peace in my life Raj … I am not complete without him … Though I know I can win over the entire world, I just can't win him back after what all I did to him." My angry face didn't change any of her frozen expressions.

She carried on as I just waited for more with my head resting on my cupped palm "I got married to a very successful guy, very rich, smart and money-minded like me. I thought together we would conquer the entire world."

"And you outsmarted him as well, as you always boss around?" I had no sympathy for this piece of disgusting shit sitting next to me.

"Yes I did and I would always do … and I would always loose every time I win. That's my punishment."

"…" I waited for more of her self-pity act to follow, all set not to buy even a single word of it.

"I still remember the date … It was June 10th and the day was Tuesday. My married life had already gone for a toss because of our fights on our careers and aspirations as to who was screwing whose life and in what all possible ways."

That's much better … So you actually got back what you gave to Mayank. I love it.

"We were vying for the same deal from the same client and our presentations were scheduled the same day; mine in the afternoon and his in the morning. We dined on the same table, slept on the same bed and came out of the same house. Yet the wall that we had built between ourselves was way too high above the bridge of our nuptial bond."

Tears rolled down her cheeks and, despite all my hatred, I felt the first surge of sympathy for her.

"There was nothing like a bonding of soul mates; we were only solitary mates; forcing checkmates to each other."

It was one of those rare occasions when I feel good about my laid back attitude in life.

The engine of the plane came to life as it started humming and grunting. I put my plans of throwing her into the nozzle on hold for some time.

She raised her voice a few octaves, trying to drown out the grunting noise of the take off.

"He gave me a call after his presentation was over, not to wish me a good day or to say anything that a husband says to his wife ... but just to taunt and brag about how cool his presentation went."

"I had no answers because I always justified to myself that life is all about winning and being on the top of the castle of the remains of your rivals. I couldn't sulk or complain. I had crafted my own fate and this was my war against me."

"Women can never think straight ... they always make things too complex and curvy ... like their own bodies." I felt like cracking this joke to lighten up the air, but it was no occasion for that.

She was speaking so dryly as if reading from a manuscript, that too without any emotions.

"I had to loose in any case … either from my soul mate or from myself." She paused to clear her throat.

"And I proved selfish again … I gave in my best shot to my presentation and rest was as I had expected… The deal was clinched by our company."

I could feel the devilish adrenalin rush pumping in her veins. I hated her again.

"I went back home and I saw him there, sprawled on the sofa, eyes buried in the ground. I was happy to make another man cry, I cared a damn even if it was 'My man'."

"'So are you going to leave me...,' he was almost begging now. But I could not see his tears as my eyes were filled with the glamour and the fame of the things coming my way."

"I was too bad, I know that, so much so that I never said to him 'I am leaving you.' I always pissed him off with my taunts and kept pushing him over the brink."

The plane was over the clouds now. I was just wondering where Mayank would have felt himself and his confidence to be ... bottom low.

"I never wanted to be blamed for being the one who walked off... My success had started making me feel that he was too straightforward and simple to be at par with my capabilities. I did not want him in my life now ... No way ... Just go Mayank ... I need a change."

You definitely do ... I need to start telling the entire world what kind of bitch you are to change the way they think.

"He embraced me when I was shattered and he was going on cloud number nine and I left him when he needed me the most.

But you know what Raj ... our deeds never leave us alone. They follow us wherever we go and we have to pay the price if we make someone cry." She was talking to herself now.

For the rest of the flight, none of us spoke a single word, there was nothing to be said at all.

Instead of the expression of "Home Sweet Home", it was the wish of "Home Neat Home" that came straight out of my heart. It was a bitter aroma of the pungent smelling bleaching powder that hit my nostrils as I took my first flight of escalators. The escalators got stuck in the middle as if encouraging you to strengthen your muscles. If that was not enough, I was greeted by a housekeeping staff who was puffing off smoke rings from his Indian Cigar (the conical paradigms of handicraft) and had one tucked neatly behind his ear.

I was already feeling pukish; resting my luggage trolley next to the waiting lounge chairs, I entered the washroom.

For a moment I thought that I had entered the art gallery of some famous artist till I realized that the apparent pieces of modern art were the random disarrayed distribution of the red spit of our own countrymen, too restless to reach the sink and so letting it go way before that.

Appreciating a great piece of "The Mona Lisa", vaguely appearing on the corner of the room, I settled myself in front of one of the piss boxes where one line was drawn. Above it, there was an advisory note written.

"If you can shoot from your hose above this; welcome to our fire brigade." All I could do was smirk and appreciate the reach and spread of the Information revolution.

I turned my head to the left to read the next message in queue... It was even more amazing ... "Shake well after use."... "Eeeeeew!" I did my best not to exclaim in mock anger.

I zipped and packed my hose and just could not suppress the urge of taking a look at the one on the right as well... It was the one that stole the show for sure.

"Would you mind looking at your own…?" I had to almost run now.

Life was slowly returning to normal... The orientation program to make you feel you are back in India was doing wonders. Who says the planning in our country is not proper?

I was trying to get over the shock and went to a snack bar to get myself a bottle of water. It was then that my phone rang. I was so restless with the "Rest room thoughts" that I just affixed it to my ears as if it was an oxygen mask.

"Welcome back to India sir, how are you feeling after spending first few minutes???" It was Nayana, I smiled for the first time and then felt sorry as well for not calling her first thing upon arrival.

"I am great dear ... Just the acclimatization is going on…" I glanced back at the restroom and commented.

"Hummmm .... So when is the Greek God going to oblige me with a small meeting?" She chuckled at the other end.

"Meeting??" So she wants to meet me actually!!! Nah ... must be only a formal gesture of welcome.

"Yeah, surely will do ... but the pleasure would be mine." I tried to sound like a perfect gentleman.

We talked for few more minutes before I started hearing the beeps of another call on my phone; it was Mom calling. I excused myself from Nayana.

"*Chintu*, where are you *beta* … your flight landed half an hour back!!"

"Yes mom ... coming ... I was in the last row, so it took some time to get out." My quiver was never short of lies.

I quickly collected my check-in bag from the luggage trolley after some trouble because all the blue bags looked the same there.

Strolling past the vulture gaze of the custom officers, I started looking for mom and dad in the crowd of anxious faces, looking anxiously for their respective international arrivals.

After spotting the pair of anxious eyes which were looking for me, I quickly marched and touched their feet. Mom had the same comment for me which she always gave me "You have lost too much weight" and Dad as usual didn't say much apart from asking about my work and future plans afterwards.

While leaving the airport, on the connecting tunnel to the parking lot, I still had to see the last of the surprises.

A bunch of cows were peacefully standing in the midway; I was sure one of them was discussing about the fodder scam with two of her other acquaintances.

Chapter 13: The Name is Bond, Family Bond

After a long onsite, a week's trip to the hometown is as necessary as abusing your supervisor after the appraisal process is over. Behind his back, of course.

I was no exception to this ritual and I was in my home town in Allahabad next day when I landed from Greece.

By the theory of relativity, Allahabad looks as serene and rustic as compared to Delhi, as Delhi looks after a long-term stay in NYC. Laid back people with no fear of looming deadlines and client commitments. Lazy afternoons which unwind at their own leisurely pace. No business at the speed of no thought - Simple!!

It was one of those relaxed evenings when I was relaxing with mom and dad when one of Dad's friends joined us for tea.

After the exchange of pleasantries and greetings, came the usual question from his side, "So *Beta,* what do you do in Delhi?"

"Uncle, I am working in SCT ... it's a S/W firm." I tried my level best to explain it to him but his facial expression revealed that he must have thought of me as a CD/DVD store employee.

But he quickly wiped those expressions off his face and shot the next arrow from his quiver... "So son, what do you make in your factory then?"

I looked back at dad with my SOS appeal. I mean, taking it as a manufacturing job is still ok, but FACTORY??

Dad somehow handled the situation and said, "No Guptajee, he is more into technical side, I mean writing programs for big foreign banks to boost up their business."

"Bravo Dad!!!" ... Simple words - Deep Impact. Kudos to you.

But making Gupta uncle understand was like making Bangladesh win against Australia on the bouncy tracks of Perth. He nodded his head vertically, though I knew the implicit nod was a horizontal one.

"So can you do me a favour Raj, I know you can do with your skills…?" he asked me.

Finally what all has been told is making sense to him, cool. I was both excited and filled with the pride of being a s/w professional.

"Actually my bank is not updating my passbook correctly, there is a credit excess of 44 rupees. Can you program something to fix that?"

He was merciless in the way he blew the bubble of my pride. I just excused myself and disappeared into the washroom. When I came back, Gupta Uncle had left.

Mom was all set and seated on the sofa... I knew that she was in the mood for having a big discussion.

"Not now Mom ... please!!" I thought ... wanting desperately to rest my tired body on the bed.

She was not at all interested in my excuses ... like a magician ... she slipped her hand inside a plastic bag and came out with a bunch of cards in them.

"Mom, what is that now...?" I said, thumping down on my knees, puzzled and confused.

The magician now shone in the glory of her artwork ... waving the hands artistically to lay all the cards on the glass table.

The expression on her face was that of a winner who had just unfolded the blind to show a series of all the aces.

The expression on mine was of someone who was entering the casino for the first time, a novice, unable yet to understand the complex games of fate.

The postcards laid on the table were actually playing cards, the only difference being that all of them were queens of all colours.

Some in saris, some in suits and a few in jeans as well ... some chuckling with their hands stylishly put on their chins and some obliging the camera with their forced smile.

So the trap was all set to get me tied in the nuptial knot.

I was in no mood for this ... how can I start my life like this ... I can't do this ... I need time.

All these expression came on to my face and left one by one ... But the only question mom had in her eyes was "Which one??"

I retorted meekly ... "Mom how can I start my life with a complete stranger, that too now...? I am only 26."

She was a merciless executioner that night... She tightened the noose even more and said..."You are right Chintu *beta*, your dad and I knew each other from our kindergarten days and shared our lunch, right *jee*?" She turned her head towards dad.

I turned to see dad's reaction ... But there was none ... I knew even then that if the foreign minister doesn't agree, he can't intervene into the home minister's portfolio.

Still I gave it a try... "Dad, please ask mom to keep it on hold for some time ... isn't it too early?"

The way dad helplessly glanced back at me, I got the silent answer that was loud and clear "Son, you can't appeal in High Court against the rulings of the Supreme Court."

My trial had ended even before it started.

The noose was too tight to plead for forgiveness from the judge.

"Ok mom, this one…" I just placed my index finger on one of the snaps. I didn't even bother to see the face. it was the loud red background that appealed more.

"You are so sweet my Chintu ... good boy ... love you." Mom just tweaked my nose and combed my hair with her fingers.

I quietly had my dinner and tried to force myself to sleep but all in vain. I kept on turning over and hid my face tightly in the pillow.

It was then that I thought about her. About Nayana!!

I felt even worse about next day's visit ... I know we are not engaged ... I know we haven't even seen each other ... leave alone being in love.

So what right do I have to say NO to marriage...? I don't even know whether she loves me ... All I know is that she was always there for me when I was away from everyone and in a country of strangers.

But should I ask her once...? Boy, what if she says yes and then she comes to know that I am looking out for the perfect bride for me. Where is this all going?

My chain of thought was broken by an SMS that glowed on my cell's screen. I knew it was Nayana... The message read:

"I knw u mst b thnkng abt ths mad girl nw...

busy talkng to mom n dad...??

dnt wry,..cl me l8r

I had my dnr, u sleep well! Good night"

She knew me too well ... and what was I thinking ... but is that enough to decide whether she is my soul mate? It was just an urge to stay in touch. But it could be out of the feelings of being left alone in an alien country and nothing else.

I don't remember when I could finally fall sleep.

Next morning I woke up with a headache. While having the sips of hot tea, it was a sweet message from Nayana that put the things back on track.

"Dnt thnk too mch abt me

We do wot v r destined to!

Hv a nice day and kp smiling!"

I kept on staring at the screen with a smile till my trance was broken by mom coming out of the kitchen and serving me a big bowl of *pakodas*.

The rich aroma of the delicacy had not even made its way all the way up to my nostrils when my mom issued her latest commandment.

"*Beta* get ready, we are going to see Amrita today!!" she said, picking up the cup of tea from the table.

The piece of *pakoda* was still halfway down its way, waiting to land in my mouth. Nayana's SMS was still open and it read "We do what we r destined to."

I wrote back…

"Hey Nayana...don't sound too philosophical!!

I am going out for a movie with mom n dad"

I unwillingly resigned to the games of destiny and got up to get ready. I was in mood to, although.

We reached the given address at around 4:00 in the evening. We were given as warm a welcome as was given to our team in the World Cup. Although I knew the results were going to be also the same. Kicked out in two rounds!!

I entered the room, flanked by mom and dad on either side as the medieval kings were escorted by their armour clad guards…

For the first few minutes, nobody spoke a word. I and the ultra shy girl were the centre of attraction as everyone glanced at us.

At that time the hush in the room was broken by an SMS that echoed throughout the room. I sent my thanks to Nayana for at least shutting the bays of wide open mouths.

"Hey Greek God!!

Howz the movie....loving it??"

"Complete bore and anticlimax..." I quickly replied and closed the flap of my cell.

"Message from the office ... Even in the holidays they don't leave you ...you know…" I tried my best to force a smile and make everyone feel easy.

"Yes. Yes!! We do understand the pressure of work *Beta,* After all Amrita also has to go through a lot of these things, right *beta*?" Now all eyes focused back to the 'touch me not'.

I don't know whether it was my fluttering eyes or the shockwave from an earthquake but I felt as if her whole body was trembling. The head was still glued to her neck.

"Yes..." She murmured so lightly as if there was some tax imposed in case you raised your voice above few octaves.

I had complete sympathy with that poor thing as I could see that her mom had almost pushed her on the edge of the bed by constant nudging of her elbows.

"So what are your hobbies and interests like?" I said in an attempt to lighten the air and make her relaxed.

Now her father also joined in pushing her on the edge of the bed. She was scratching the floor with her toenails so hard that she surely could dig at least one oil well overnight.

"She is excellent at cooking ... And she paints real well...,".came the proxy replies from her mom and dad.

I really did not know what else to ask as I was sure she was almost on the verge of a nervous breakdown.

After sipping down the tea and 'home made' *samosas*, I was all set to move as mom was pinching me too hard beneath the disguise of her folded hands.

On the stairs, Amrita's elder sister ran past me and made a complete road block with her spread hands.

"So ... when do you think you'd be getting married...? You didn't even ask anything from Amrita?"

I had nothing to ask. Not because I did not like the girl but since making a decision based on a single meeting was like predicting the result of a cricket match on the very first ball delivered.

"Actually mom would talk to you about this ... I cannot decide on my own." The dryness in my voice made the barriers hang loose and I fled past quickly.

But she was not going to let me off so easily. "So what is your nick name Raj ... what does your mom call you?"

That sounded like a pretty harmless question, so I replied with a mild smile "Mom calls me Chintu!!"

"You know what, we call Amrita Chinti because she eats very little ... See it rhymes so well … Chintu and Chinti ... you would definitely make a great pair after marriage."

I was flabbergasted at her match-making abilities ... I thought of my best friend from school, Anurag whose nickname was Pintu. By her logic, should I be tying the knot with every Pintu and Mintu??

"I would call an auto to go back." I tried very hard to maintain the smile on my lips and before it could slip down, I briskly walked to leave her standing on the stairs.

I was thinking real hard on the way back. Am I going to start my life with a complete stranger on the basis of how good her culinary and fine arts skills are?

OR with someone who at least knows me for the last so many months ... who is not just another chat ID in the virtual world neither someone who knows only my a/s/l details.

The auto took the last turn into my street. "We know each other's likes and dislikes ... But does she really like me…?"

The auto stopped with a jerk and a screech of the brakes and so did my chain of thoughts. "DO I LIKE HER?"

"Chintu ... do you have a 10 rupee note ... I do not have..." Mom was busy looking, frisking her bag, and dad had walked to unlock the door.

I handed the note to the driver and slowly closed the gate behind.

"I cannot close all the doors of fate on me ... at least not without making a knock on it." My heavy legs were getting steadied as they might have received the hint towards the right path to walk on.

My head was spinning with the web of intertwining thoughts of "She loves me … She loves me not…" I gently rested my head on the pillow.

"Chintu, have food and then go to sleep *beta*." Mom opened the door ajar and called me.

I was not listening to what she said. The words hit the drums of my ear but reached nowhere.

"I am NOT going to let it go as another story which starts with an e-greeting of "I love you sweetheart" and ends with an SMS of "It's not working for us".

I picked up my cell and did something I always shied away from; confronting the situation in the real word. I typed a message to Nayana.

"I want to know what the destiny has in store for us.

Can we meet on Tuesday morning when I come back to Delhi?"

I lay down again.

I probably dozed off for an hour because, when I woke up, I realized that my room's light was switched off and all I could hear was the sound of the washing of utensils from the kitchen.

I looked back at my cell which flashed no new messages on screen!! May be I was getting too optimistic about Nayana. She must have thought me as some despo, jumping way too early to conclusions of she being head over heels for me.

Mom entered the room again and placed a glass of milk on the table and mumbled "No lunch ... No dinner ...at least have some milk and break your fast."

I didn't feel any hunger or thirst. So I just pulled up the sheet over my head. I and my darkness make the perfect match.

Mom got really irritated. "And you didn't even tell me that you are travelling back to Greece again ... that's why you are not serious about marriage also, right?"

I sat up in the bed, confused and irritated, "Now who told you that I am travelling back to Greece?"

"I just read your message ... Your travel manager wants to meet you on Monday morning 10:00 'o clock in Janpath ... now you have started hiding things Chintu?"

The sad expressions on my face quickly got alt+tabbed to a large grin and I almost screamed at the top of my voice. "Mom ... I am very hungry ... give me something NOW."

Behind me, I heard mom's voice disappearing in thin air. "Mad boy ... What is so bad in India that he doesn't want to be here?"

I thanked God; He has His own strange ways of crafting our fates.

Chapter 14: Meeting Nayana

I was eagerly waiting for her to come from the other side of the road. Suddenly there was a tap on my shoulders and I turned around to see the face that I was destined to see for the rest of my life. It was so windy that day that her entire face was getting covered by her curly hair, every now and then.

"Raj?? Hi!!, I am Nayana." She didn't crack any jokes regarding the travel manager or the Greek god and, by George, her warm voice felt so smooth that it actually melted down the alley of my heart.

But it was definitely not love at first sight. Because she didn't give me enough time to catch a sight of her face the first time I saw her. By the time I could allow my eyes to scroll down from her big and talkative eyes, she quickly turned and marched inside MacD. I was whacked by the first aftershocks of the lady in red, not in mood but suit.

McD couples are like railway's general compartment passengers ... you are not welcome when you break into their space, but soon you become so much a part of it that you don't know whose cheese you are dipping your fries into.

She stopped at the counter and I thought that maybe now I might get a better view of the beautiful lips that were not coming to rest like the rest of her body.

She was nibbling, chewing or pursing them but some restless chain of thoughts was not letting them to come to peace.

My eyes were still dangling at her upper lip, all set to trek down to the lower one, when she turned around to move out, saying "There is no place for us to sit."

I looked at a number of vacant chairs lying every here and there, then back to my attire -- wasn't shabby, tried to sniff my deo -- wasn't bad, and consciously ran my fingers in my hair -- well combed. What's wrong?

I was getting nervous and loosing heart. "What's wrong Raj, why is she running away from you? I am really good for nothing, I shouldn't waste anymore time of ours."

But it would have been an unforgivable crime to take leave from the beautiful lady like this. So I put my best jogger shoes forward to match with her brisk pace.

Shouldering past the morning crowd of CP, I was almost running after her, and then she came to a halt all of a sudden and turned back to face me.

My body silently abided by Newton's first law and didn't come to a halt as I had wished it to. Her palm quickly rose up to my chest to stop me. For a few moments I was dancing on my toes like a carried away fielder on the boundary line, trying his best not to touch the rope.

Then it felt like as if time had come to a halt. I could never believe that I was actually seeing her so closely. The big eyes were fathoming for something in my eyes.

The lips were still now, as if they had found the place to rest on and where they really belonged, I thought wishfully.

But I couldn't believe what I got to hear from her as the first official statement about us.

She almost screamed, "I hate you and never in my life, have I seen a cheap guy like you, who do you think you are Raj??"

My reaction was as pathetic as that of the boundary line fielder who is shown a boundary signal by the umpire despite all his pleadings of "I didn't touch the rope".

I had nothing much to say. I was standing too close to her to even join my hands and ask for forgiveness, but for what?

Yet, she didn't stop staring into my eyes, that made me too nervous apart from the glances of passersby who were generously appreciating our 'Fevicol' posture.

Suddenly, the tightened lips relaxed into a gentle smile and she said, "Why didn't you meet me earlier? I was too nervous because I didn't know how to say that, so I was just running around!!"

The hot 'n cold treatment was so sudden and shocking that I couldn't stop exhaling a big gasp of exhilaration to absorb the tremors she gave me.

"Seriously Raj, I have seen enough of all kinds of sadistic and selfish persons all through my life and here you are, so nice and amazing, yet so real." The smile had turned into a childlike chuckle.

"But how much do you know me Nayana? I mean this the first time we are meeting," I eased myself by withdrawing myself from the 'Silly point' position and we started walking on.

"Raj, sometimes you don't get to know a person even after spending your entire life and sometimes even a casual glance says it all," she said, staring down at the road.

"Well, quite right... Its not about how many moments of life you spend, it's about how much life is there in each moment,"

I smiled back at her as if comparing the relative gravity of our statements.

"Mr Raj, that is a stolen quote from somewhere, now shut up and tell me where we are having our lunch, aren't you hungry??" She winked at me.

"I am famished ... let's go to the restaurant on the other side of the road. I really love the *Chole bhature* there!" I lied since I had never been to this restaurant ever in my life.

I just wanted to hold her hand by any excuse; crossing the road was just one of them.

I was too eager in my monkey act as I jumped and shouted like one, "Watch out!!! Bus!!" and I clutched her arm, didn't I like it?

"Raj, easy ... the bus is far away, and you know what, it just pulled over at the stop!!" She looked really concerned for me.

I felt like banging my head on the wall but there was none so I dropped the idea and quickly hid my hands in my trouser pockets.

"No I insist Raj, we WILL take the subway." She held my index finger as if taking a small kid for a walk.

If you could ignore the traces of bleaching powder's smell, the subway was a cool and pleasant change from the scorching heat outside.

I don't know if it was the effect of the darkness or a wild imagination of my own vivid thoughts, but I felt as if she got really close to me and her shoulder kept on brushing my shoulder all the way.

I tried my level best to squint in the darkness, but all I could feel was the fragrant aroma of her hair. Or was it just my own thoughts.

I must be day dreaming, I just shrugged off my thoughts and smiled back at her as she neatly tucked her long hair with a clip.

We entered the restaurant and I quickly eyed one corner table and suggested "That one is right under the AC, shall we?"

There were three chairs around the table; I quickly put my jacket on the corner one so that we could sit next to each other.

"Am I being too desperate on the very first date, just because she said I am too nice, did I take that as I love you!!" I just shrugged off the idea.

"I want two plates of *chole bhature*, I have heard that it is too delicious at your restaurant!" I was too happy to see that her hunger had kept her oblivious of my silly acts.

"Ma'am! Ours is a Chinese restaurant... We don't serve *chole bhature* here, I am so sorry. Shall I get you the menu ma'am?" The waiter replied promptly.

Nayana looked back at me with mock anger. For a moment I felt if I could dig a pit right beneath the table and live there for the rest of my life, I would.

"That's ok Raj, all the places in CP look alike, no wonder you got easily confused." She consoled me and gently squeezed my fingers with her palms.

Well, for that kind of consolation, I don't mind making this mistake every now and then, I thought.

"Raj, I am not feeling easy, I will just wash my face and come back," she declared, drumming the table with her fork, like a kid.

"Ok dear, go and cool yourself." I smiled and stood from my chair to let her go.

"Raj, are you an idiot?" She again said tersely.

I was never treated like this by someone who I met for the first time. However, there was something uncanny about her that didn't make me feel insulted.

"When with a lady, you should escort her to door of the washroom, especially if it is at such a deserted place." She softened her tone to almost a mew.

I followed her all the way up and down the stairs. She went up smiling but on the way back she was annoyed.

'Must be an unclean place, girls are so particular about such stuff,' I quickly thought.

We had our lunch; having casual chats about my onsite experiences and her attempts to switch to a better job.

Coming out, I tried to keep the conversation rolling and asked "Why do you want to switch to a different job, not happy with the current one?" I broke the fortune cookie, wondering what fortune had in store for me.

"Since it does not allow me to watch a movie as and when I want, do you understand?" Her familiar grin was back again.

"What? Do you want to watch a movie now??" I quickly calculated that the movie would be over by 6:00 in the evening and then she would leave for home. When would we find some time to talk?

"Yes, sure! Which movie do you want to see by the way?" I wiped out the frustration and tried my best to sound chirpy.

"I would love to go for *Cliff hanger*, Sylvester is my favourite, and there is a show at 3:40 in PVR, shall we?" She handed me a pamphlet of the movie schedule.

"Is she here to watch a movie??" I had definitely made a very bad impression upon her from the very beginning ... I guess she was too embarrassed to say that on my face, so she was just shunning me away."

The movie started and we got seats in the last row, not because we looked like a couple in love but because very few had turned up for this movie, boring and stale like me, I thought.

I rested on my push back seat to enjoy the next few hours. If Stallone was hanging from the cliff then even I was being pushed to the edge by her.

After few minutes of the movie had rolled past, I felt as if she was looking at me. I thought it's my own hallucination and the stretch of imagination.

But she was again looking into my eyes, her head tilted on her and real close to my shoulders. I felt really at the end of my wits and really didn't know how to react.

"Raj, you are not only a cheap guy, you are also as stupid as possible. What do you think you are doing?" She said in a choked voice, she was sobbing.

I was really scared. I had understood that I was not the perfect date material, but what did I do to bring about this catastrophe?

I was blabbering, really not knowing how to console her. "I will leave now ... I am really sorry Nayana, I know I have not talked properly to you and acted too idiotically ... I ...I will..."

I don't know what made the deeper impact, the shrieks of the onscreen lady falling into the deep gorge or the slap on my cheeks that shook my head.

Yes, she hit me, and hit real hard. Thanks to the surround sound effect nobody in the hall heard it.

"Raj, you are not worth loving any one, neither anybody should love you ... How do I make you understand what I am trying to tell you for ages?" Her fingers had not left my cheeks yet, though they had curled a bit and I felt the sting of her nails.

"..." I was in mute mode. Her thumb on my lips and shocked state of my mind didn't allow me to say a single word.

"I have kept on staring at you to show that the only thing I have in my eyes is you ... I took you through the subway and to the washroom because I thought your hesitation would go away when we were alone." She dug her nails harder.

"Don't you even hear what every heartbeat of mine wants to tell you?" She gently gripped my hand and placed it over the pulse of her throbbing heart beats, humming in tandem with mine.

I don't remember who made the first move. It was not important either because we both were wanting it to happen.

I don't even know what kept on pulling us to each other but we just abided by the magic spell till our parted lips got a snug fit for themselves.

The soft touch of it kindled a fire which slowly melted our stiffening and slithering bodies into a soothing hug.

I scratched my cheek and, with mock anger, I ran my fingers where she had dug her nails.

She turned my faced towards her and planted kisses on each of them.

Never in my life had I felt so complete when she rested her head on my shoulders and nudged it with her nose.

Chapter 15: The Hand that Stabs the Back

"No, I don't agree with you Nayana... I am not going to talk to that jerk Sundeep?". I sipped my coffee so fast that it burnt my tongue and left me sulking.

"What's wrong with you? Why don't you talk it out rather than curse and blame your fate for it."

I had told Nayana about the steal-the-deal act of Mayank and now I was in no mood for a faceoff with him which she was encouraging me to undertake.

"I don't want to discuss it any more or any further. I am sick of that ba...," I was getting really carried away when she gestured to me to keep mum.

"I know you have a very rich vocabulary of adjectives but save it for some other time," she taunted and it hurt me real deep.

"So what do you want, I should have a round table meeting with the guy who screwed my dreams and my career to the hilt?" I tried to sound as dry as possible.

"Yes, because then only he would realize that what it meant for you ... and Raj, you never know what the complete story is..." She reached out and clasped my wrist with her fingers.

"Ok, Nayana ... I will do it only for you. We gotta go now," I stood up from my chair and got ready to move.

"Believe me Raj, you would surely feel better after discussing it over with him..." She patted my arms. "And let's go, it's already 8:45."

As I dropped her in front of her office, she turned my face towards her and said, "Always have a faceoff with the situations and people rather than making assumptions."

I nodded my head and drove to my office.

As I parked my bike in the office parking lot, I was in no mood to talk to Mayank. Anyway the mail for approval and QPM implementation plan was about to come from the client today.

'I would lie to Nayana, what is the big deal in saying that Mayank was not game for a talk?' I thought, hanging my helmet from the handle as I was about to hang this issue in middle of nowhere.

As I was about to enter the office, I saw Mayank in the breakout area, with his body leaned comfortably against the wall, smoking, relaxed and scanning his favourite section of the crowd.

I didn't know what took me over completely and I walked up straight to him. "Hi Mayank, all set for the big day?"

"Big day?" He woke up from his deep concentration... "Oh, you mean the QPM thing, *yaar*. That is meant for big shots like you, who toiled so hard to make the whole thing possible."

"But smart and shrewd work is way better and rewarding than hard work, isn't it Mayank?" I wanted to see the changing colours of his face, but he just threw the stub on the ground and crushed it under his shoes.

"Lets go and have some cold drink man, you seem to be badly hit by the heat" He mocked my frustration and held me by my shoulders as I started to walk towards my cubicle.

I shook my head in "NO" first, however my hatred for him got better of my "let it go" attitude again. I walked up to him and said, "Can we go to cafeteria Mayank? I want to discuss something over the cold drink to cool off my head!!"

"Is she not letting you kiss her, see what I suggest is..." his broad grin froze and dropped as he saw my blank face. "Ok, give me two seconds, I will just check my mails..." I dragged my lifeless legs to follow him inside the office, he could delay the conversation but I wanted a closure today by all means.

"As if you don't know what's in there?" I stared and barked at him as he did the three fingers act to unlock his PC. All I got back was a confused smile and a meaningless wink.

"By the way Raj, why are you so cold about QPM, I mean look at you, in Greece you were so mad that you even missed some late night religious shows..." My cold reaction again snapped him quiet.

"Ok boss!! So the much awaited QPM mail has arrived! mmmmmm ... let me open the mother of all projects!!" He hummed something happily and clicked open the mail.

I didn't even care to look at his monitor since I knew what was in there and the reaction was about to get painted on his face.

"What the hell..." His mouth was open ajar as he gestured to me with both his hands to have a look at the monitor.

"Why are you acting innocent Mayank, as if I don't know?" I bent down to have a closer look at the monitor and read what I had discovered 2 months ago.

FROM: GREEKO BANK

"We are pleased to announce that the QPM initiative pioneered by SCT is accepted at GCS and the rollout of the first phase is scheduled to begin in September.

The credit goes to the entire team involved in this initiative but due to the diligent and dedicated work, we wish to offer our special thanks to Mr Sundeep Lal, who prepared the plan and proposal and would lead the QPM development team."

"Sundeep!!" For a few moments, the only sound that we could hear was of the key chain that was dangling from my mouth.

We stared at the monitor for so long that the "clouds" screensaver started floating on the monitor, and as it scattered and demystified, so did my thoughts.

So this is how he did it. Since Mayank was never too serious about the QPM presentation, he must have detached his presentation and used his own name instead.

I turned my face to Mayank, who was in the same state of shock.

"You should have never sent your mails from Sundeep's machine." I hated calling him "Sandy" now.

"What are you talking man, what mails and why from his PC!!" His lips were still parted like the Bay of Bengal and his eyes were fixed on the mail.

"When your mail set-up was not ok for about a week and you used his machine to send mails." I tried to tweak his memory.

"Raj, it never happened and by the way..." He turned his revolving chair towards me."...how do YOU know about it, you were never there when Sundeep was in Greece?"

"He only told me." I said, realizing that something was really wrong.

After 10 minutes I was done telling him the whole story.

"Oh, that is why your behaviour was so weird and bitter in those last few months?" I could feel the hint of irritation and anger in his voice.

"Raj, I know I am not a very nice guy, I flatter my bosses a lot for my own selfish motives, but why would I play with someone else's dreams and ambitions??"

I had no answers. I was looking down into the ground.

"On top of everything Raj, why didn't you discuss it over with me, WHY NOT?"

I remembered what Nayana told me in the morning. "Always have a faceoff with … rather than making assumptions."

"I know Mayank, I have been a complete jerk, I assumed everything rather than..."

At that moment, the swinging door to our area was yanked open by Ganesh, followed by Sundeep. The way Ganesh was giving a smile of appreciation to Mayank, I knew that the news was already out.

"You know, Raj ... Mayank, Sandy has fetched the big QPM deal for SCT, he is such a cool and silent killer!!"

'Silent killer?? Back stabber might be a better address for him.' I thought.

"Yes Ganesh, he is really good at making the best use of resources, so well that even the resources don't get to know that they are being used!" Mayank cribbed and took a step forward.

As usual, Ganesh nodded his head without understanding even a word of it and headed for his seat.

And now the three of us were left. Mayank stood up with his fists clenched but I gestured to him to stop right there. This was neither the right way, nor the right place.

The face that had once reminded me of a monk, looked like that of a cold-blooded murderer today.

He walked up with a smirk on his face and said, "Raj, I told you, it's a jungle out there!! Didn't I warn you my dear?"

Mayank was fuming with anger and he exploded again, "Don't you have any ethics Sundeep, do you understand what you have done?"

"The jungle has no rules or ethics sweetheart, and look who is talking about morals, Mr Casanova." Sundeep gently pushed down the dagger and it did make Mayank bleed.

The viper in the monk's robe hissed again, "I knew you are too carefree and can easily get carried away with situation. Since you were going on so well with the QPM thing that I knew I had no other way but to kill your enthu and steal the deal!"

"But what about that mail Sundeep, Mayank had never sent that mail!" I knew we were knocked out, still I wanted to know when I got the killer punch.

"Easy tiger, I am coming to that." The crooked smile was not ready to go... "It was a trap that might not have worked, but it did, and just the way I wanted it."

I was restlessly shaking my legs and Mayank was clutching the handles of his chair so hard as if he wanted to uproot them right away! Both were waiting for the crooked act to be unveiled.

Giving us a patronizing look, he continued, "I took an old mail of mine, edited the contents to make it look like it was sent by Mayank and saved it as a draft. The only risk I took was to put it in my "Sent" folder with my "Outlook skills" to make it look like a sent one and wait for you to come and take the bait!!"

Mayank and I sat in silence. We had nothing to say.

All I could think of was, "If only I had discussed the matter with Mayank once at least."

Sundeep made the finishing touches to his masterpiece and said, "I didn't win since I was the best, but I won since I was the only one running."

This time Mayank broke past the barricades of my hands. Pointing his index finger and thumb like a pistol, he pushed it against Sundeep's chest, "You are going to pay for what you have done!"

Sundeep wiped off his hands like dirt and said, "You can never ever be a threat for me and Raj...," he turned on his heels and said, "I am going to take good care of him."

"Good care???" He left me hanging in the hooks of a lot of question marks when he calmly walked past and made himself comfy on his chair.

"What does he mean??" I was really tense.

I and Mayank were cornered in the "Kudos Party" thrown in the evening by Ganesh. All our zapped faces could do were to sip on our drinks and watch the ugly jig of the madly drunk pig named Sundeep.

Chapter 16: The Job Hopper

The chain of events shook me so much that I had hardly any affection left for the SCT group or my work.

So I decided to Hop -- the act usually undertaken for the clink of the money or for adding wings to your career. In my case, it was the unprofessional song I wasn't any more willing to sing.

It is the easiest and the toughest job to identify the person who is striving hard for a switch and appearing in round after round of telephonic interviews. Toughest since the breakout areas is always full of dozens of guys and gals clinging to their phones and picking the job hopper out of them is very much like searching for a needle in the hay.

But it becomes a little easier after some careful observations. Someone talking to his/her respective would have smiles and chuckles on their faces, cupping their faces every now and then, maybe to blow a kiss or say something really intimate.

Whereas a job seeker looks really like an object of pity ... wiping their face every now and then ... Sometimes looking up to the heavens with eyes closed and sometimes at his toes, as if the answer is lying locked somewhere down below.

Incidentally, when I became one, I never wanted to be spotted like one so I decided to go for an alternate solution. I decided to give the interviews in a car. I didn't have one so I had to borrow one from Sharat, an old acquaintance who I met through a common friend.

Sharat Holker was quite a character. He was basically from Mumbai but did his schooling from Punjab and then stayed in Tamilnadu for his engineering. I could never understand whether his weird behaviour was due to this blend of so many varied hues of experiences or something else. But due to that only we used to call him "S. Holker" with a little relaxed pronunciation of the initial."

I still remember the date... It was 26th May and I had the interview scheduled for 2:00 in the afternoon. I came to office in the morning and started mugging up the concepts and all the other relevant details.

I used the Alt+Tab as and when someone passed by to hide what all I was doing...

As the clock struck 1:50, I walked down to Sharat and asked for his keys. Came back the prompt query.

"For how may kilometres you are going to drive today...?" He asked without raising his head.

"Sharat, I just want to drive down to the bank." That used to be my all-time favourite excuse.

"Why can't you take an auto or rickshaw man...? The bank is just round the corner, isn't it?" he said, adjusting his half moon glasses.

I looked at my watch. It was 1:55 now. Do something Raj ... only last 5 minutes to go.

"Its damn hot out there Holker Sir ... please if you could do me this favour." I was everything but down on my knees.

"Ummmmmmmmmm ... ok you take it ... but get it refuelled for 100 bucks..." He finally expressed his intentions.

'100 bucks for two kilometres ... I guess I must go to the bank five times in that case you bloody scoundrel' I thought and said "Sure man, you don't have to say that."

"1:57" ... I rushed hastily and entered the car which was no less than a furnace in the scorching afternoon. I drove it out of the office, parking it under the shade of a tree.

It was five past two now and there was no call as of yet. I was feeling irritated and opened the front windows to kill the suffocation...

It was then that the phone rang and I knew that it was for the telephonic round.

"Hi Raj, this is Tushar here... I believe we have an interview scheduled now ... is it the right time to talk?" came the stereotyped question from the other end.

A drop of sweat appeared on the back of my head; it trickled down my neck and on to my back. Did I have too many options?

"Oh definitely. Yes Tushar ... I am all set..." I said, hastily pulling up the power windows to drown out the noise from outside.

"Ok, Raj ... tell me something about yourself..."

This question always irritated me a lot ... because I never knew the perfect answer for it and wrapped it up somehow.

I gave him some gas to make it look like an answer and I was very sure that he must have put his handset aside because he knew that the answer had nothing to do with either my selection or rejection. It was one of those questions which were like rating yourself on a scale of 5 or 10.

After the exchange of few more pleasantries, came the first question.

"Raj, can you explain to me how the virtual table is created and used for virtual classes in one of your project experience?"

The heat of the closed and locked car hit the shores of my senses... I knew (had mugged up) the two answers separately but how to link them?

"Ugh ... Actually virtual table is created dynamically..." I spat whatever I remembered in an attempt to get at least half the credit.

"But Raj, my question was how you implemented this in your project work?"

"..." I tried hard but could remember only the cut, copy and paste techniques that I had used till date.

"It's ok Raj ... let's move on to next question ... tell me about the most exciting project experience you have had."

Most exciting experience! Well, that was going to the beer bars or watching late night shows after the boring office hours.

No, Raj!! Think hard ... this is the question which can be the decider ... you gotta make up something, right now.

My wet shirt was now sticking to the car seat and the heat was not allowing me to think anything else. I stepped out of the car and ran under the shelter of a big tree.

"Raj, are you with me…?" came the query and the concerned voice from the other end.

At that moment, a call centre cab sped past me, all set to hit the terminal velocity in next few seconds, honking as if it had just robbed a bank and was being chased by cops now.

"Raj ... Raj ... hello…" I could feel the irritation that had started to creep into the voice of Tushar now.

"Hi, Can you call me after 5 minutes...? There is too much noise on the line ... I don't know why..." I said with a forced giggle which sounded completely artificial.

"Ok Raj, no issues." And he hung up, I felt as if he had slammed down the phone.

From my experience, I knew that if the word "issues" is used in a discussion even if to say "no issues", that simply means there are a lot of issues.

I was sweating profusely even in the shadow of the tree ... the humid weather was killing me and I felt I would collapse at any moment.

I sat back in the car, knowing that I could not stand out in the noise and have to bear the heat. WHY I HAD TO TAKE THIS ANTIQUE PIECE OF WORK WHICH DOESN'T EVEN HAVE AN AC IN IT?

The options were few and I knew that he wouldn't call back again. So I turned the ignition on, steered the car to the left to take it to petrol pump to do the 'reimbursement' act.

It was then that the phone rang again.

"Is it ok Raj, the network seems to have improved now ... eh?" I could sniff the sarcasm in his voice.

"Yeah ... a lot clearer now..." I was not only happy since he called back but something had struck my mind in the meanwhile regarding the question he had asked.

"So can we proceed from where we left ... I asked about any exciting experience ... any initiatives that you started on your own?" He seemed a bit softer now.

"Yes I did actually! I worked for a new initiative called Quick ProM which is used for the effective portfolio management of the end clients of the bank." I shot out the whole sentence in one breath.

"So your design and technical architectures have been accepted?" He sounded impressed now by the gravity of the concepts I had presented forth.

I wiped my forehead and neck with my hanky... "Say it Raj, this can be the decider..." A voice came from inside my heart.

"Yes, actually they are about to be implemented by the end of next month." I knew I was lying, but wasn't I betrayed?

"That's amazing Raj, can you briefly explain about it, in a nutshell?" I could feel that now he had leaned forward to carefully listen to every word from me.

We talked for another 20 minutes in which I explained to him the design and implementation of QPM. When, it ended, I knew that I had won half the battle at least as I knew the ins and outs of the QPM like my baby.

"Sounds very impressive Raj, but is it possible for you to send me the presentation you had made for QPM?" He shot the last one before wrapping up.

"..." Why does he want the slides, that's confidential.

"I know Raj that this is the most unusual request you might have ever come across, but it is essential and can make your selection a sure shot."

Essential? But how? I explained everything to him in the best possible manner, why does he need a supporting document for that? The hush from my side was so long that it triggered further explanation from Tushar.

"Raj, I have interviewed 4 to 5 candidates and so have my other colleagues today. I must say that you are the one."

I basked in the glory of feeling like the Neo of the matrix for a few seconds, but the doubt was still there, Why does he want the presentation?

He carried on... "There is a chance that they might not buy my idea of you being the best candidate, and your presentation might be the best thing to make them believe what I am saying."

Hummmmm... makes sense, I thought, but sending a confidential document through office ID, it was not only unethical but also a violation of policy and could have shown me the EXIT out of SCT straight away.

"I understand your fears Raj, but I have thought of an alternate way. You send it via an anonymous ID on yahoo mail to Tusharg ... your name can never be dragged in this issue by your organization, makes sense?"

That sounded reasonable to me. "So Tushar, can I just send it across to you by tomorrow evening?"

There was a pause at the other end ... and then came the reply. "I am afraid Raj, we are finalizing everything by 6:00 PM today, you need to send it to me latest by 4:00. I can't promise much without that."

4:00PM! I took a look at my watch... It was 2:40 already. I knew that I had to attend a telephonic call which was going to start at 3:00.

"I will do that Tushar, don't worry." I knew for sure that my selection or rejection was entirely dependent on this presentation.

"Ok Raj... Great talking to you... Hope to see you soon in GlobalCon." And we hung up after that.

I was back on my seat at 2:50. Wasted another 5 minutes in convincing Sharat about why I couldn't get the petrol filled in his car.

"2:55." I was anxiously tapping my fingers on the keyboard. I opened the password protected folder in which I had stored my presentation.

"Anyway it was not selected and someone else stole the show, why should I care about being ethical?" I tried to justify my stand.

I opened a new mail, typed Tushar's address and attached my presentation.

"What if you are caught Raj?" that was the last warning call that came from inside.

"There are thousands of mails being exchanged every day... Who has the time to go through each of them?"

"Raj... The call is starting, would you mind joining us?" Ganesh shouted from his seat. So very usual of him, when would you learn some soft skills man.

The tussle was still on in my mind. "I sent so many personal mushy mails to all my chat-mates ... was I ever caught? NO!, then how come today?"

I steadied my shaking fingers on the mouse and hit the "Send" button.

Within seconds I received a failure notice from Yahoo. The mail ID given by Tushar was not valid.

Quickly I hit back the mobile number from which I got the call.

It was switched off.

I rushed for the call. Puzzled and annoyed.

Chapter 17: Murphy's Law

Next morning I woke up with a heavy head and aching body. I had a look at my watch and it was already 10:00 in the morning.

Then I recalled that I had three rounds of beer with Mayank last night. "Shit! Have I already accepted me as a looser?"

I remembered that I had promised Nayana that I would never smoke or drink again.

I clutched my spinning head. "What did God do to me for carrying out a promise for all these days?" I threw away my sheet on the floor and got up to my feet.

As I splashed cold water on my drowsy and blood red eyes, I heard my cell ringing.

"Raj where are you, I have been trying you for two hours, do you know how worried I am for you?" Nayana was screaming with all her might.

"I am sorry Nayana, I slept too late and have a very bad headache even now," I replied as mildly as possible because she was fuming now after knowing that was alive and fine and still didn't get back to her.

"Raj, what happened to your throat, did you again smoke and drink?" She said angrily. How on earth did she know everything about me?

"Nothing Nayana ... I just woke up … maybe because of that, honey." I tried to control my stammering tongue but that was a failed attempt.

"Raj, I don't know but I smell something really fishy!" There was a pause at the other end for too long and then she asked.

"Would you come to pick me up in the evening, my hero?" Thanks a bunch God, finally she smiled.

"Yes sweetie, even if I have to fly all the way to crash land in your arms, I will be there for you, love you." I relaxed for those few moments.

It was already too late for office – So I saved few buckets and mugs of water which would have instead gone waste on getting rid of my stubble and rich body aroma.

I entered the office – sleepy eyes and a dizzy head. I logged into my machine. My eyelids were getting heavier and my nauseating senses made me feel like all the eyes in office were glued on me.

"It's ok to be a little unorganized, that's the sign of a genius." -- I wanted to make them understand, but then rather preferred to take a stroll to the cafeteria; that killer feeling was too freaky for my liquor-laden body and soul.

I took a black coffee and was a little relieved to see Mayank entering from the other end of the hall. I took a big swig and washed my teeth's array with it – tastes better with un-brushed gums and tongue.

Mayank's face didn't look too amused; in fact he was looking sad and worried.

"All is well, bro?" I asked him, raising my right eyebrow up – thinking it looked impressive.

"You know what a mess you have dragged yourself into?" – He uttered – almost in a cursing tone.

I tried to recollect of any brawls or rash driving which I ended up doing last night – but my blanked out mind didn't return any output.

"What is it Mayank…?" I leaned forward to sniff the rich coffee aroma which was billowing up my nostrils.

"There is a rumour and talk in the office that you have leaked something important over the emails," Mayank said slowly, almost matching the flow of coffee vapour.

"Rumour – email – Leak…" These words made no sense to the canvas of my blank mind, but as I moved along the brush of imagination along them, the picture which came out was as scary as the Indian roads in the rains.

"What do you mean…? But how…? Are you trying … the QPM mmmmail…?" My stuttering tongue was as shaky as the coffee mug in my throbbing fingers.

"Yes -- Unfortunately this is what I mean, I am not sure what were you trying to do?" Mayank said tersely, raising his hands up in deep exasperation.

I was shell shocked; what is this and why is it happening to me?

I made some more brushstrokes on the pothole-studded road and when it took a few turns a few milestones back – I realized where I had slipped and crashed down.

Strange, I didn't even notice this! When Sundeep said *"I am going to take good care of him"* to Mayank.

"Crazy, Sick bastard…" I couldn't believe he could get down to such atrocities.

"Who are you talking about Raj?" Mayank landed the back his palms on the table with a thud.

I was too shaken to get hit or started anymore, I told him the entire story.

"Son of a bitc…" Mayank clinched his fist real tight.

"Mayank, I am sorry – I should have spoken to you about this, but now I am almost dead – He is after my career now…" I was almost in tears.

"Hey man, that's a good learning for bad times ahead, but what do we do now?"

What can be done now? I had dug myself too deep a grave to even think about a revival plan.

Suddenly my cell rang, it was Nayana. Not this time, what do you think I can talk about?

Mayank walked back to give me the privacy as I took the call.

"Hey Mr Coder … what is it so great you are working on that you haven't given me a buzz for ages?" She chuckled and giggled at the other end.

"Nothing Nayana. I am little disturbed, I will talk to you later." I had no idea how to explain the mess I had dragged myself into.

"No Raj, you can talk to me – I was just joking and pulling your leg … tell me what's wrong." Her voice changed by quite a few octaves to a serious tone.

"Nayana, you wouldn't understand the complexities of the IT world – I wish I could translate this in the BPO language which you speak." I barked and realized what I had said after a few moments.

There was a long pause at the other end, more like a blank space to fill that in with my apologies. There were none that followed though, my screwed up spirits were still inflated with arrogance.

"Well Raj, I know what cut and paste cutting edge technologies you guys work on and what sort of overselling you do for your stupid products." She stung back real hard.

"You called me stupid … you dumb bi…" I was losing control on my language.

"Yea go on, why did you stop, show what sort of an upbringing you have had, you small-town retard." Now this was going in every possible wrong direction.

"Oh Yes – that's what you big-town girls are after – A fat wallet, a dumb head and a look out for the next one." We were burning our delicately built love nest with all our ego furies.

"Are you calling me a whore…? How dare you…? You lousy punk."

The post hanging-up beeps coming from the other end didn't sadden me, I was rather clueless and lost as to what was so wrong with this day.

The phone rang again, I was in no mood to talk with this kind of temperament.

"Nayana, See we can…" But I was cut short by a male baritone voice.

"Hi, Is it Raj…?" The heavy voice almost echoed in all the corners of my ear tunnel before hitting the shores of my receptors.

"Yes… This is Raj…" I moved the phone away to glance at the screen and it was an unknown number. Is it some Tushar again?

"Raj, this is Rahul Malik here, Hope you know me – Can you meet in my cabin in the next 15-20 minutes?" The voice flew at the same gravity and pitch.

"Sure Rahul." And the call was disconnected. I was shit scared now about my career and the road ahead.

Rahul Malik – In terms of hierarchy he was the grandfather of Raghav and Ganesh (Boss's boss) and my interaction with him was limited to seeing him at the annual functions or the award distribution ceremonies.

I knew the nature and the outcome of the discussion, yet I ventured up the stairs to meet him on the first floor.

In Rahul's cabin, my replies were only limited to "Um...," "Ughh...," "Actually...," "Sorry...," and "Ok."

It took him only 6 minutes and 6 seconds to decide the abrupt ending of 6 long years of my career. No big deal as it had taken HIM the same time to close the chapter of my 6 months of love life.

I was taking the flight of the stairs when a message flashed on my screen, I opened it, it was from Nayana.

"Doesn't look like we are meant to be together.

I am leaving this place and your life and going to take up a job offer for US.

Please don't try to find me, It'd only hurt me even more."

Everything was going wrong for me, just when I wanted at least one support to bank on.

Chapter 18: The Perfect Plan

I was sitting with my head clutched between my knees ... Job ... love and my dreams, everything lost in one go and in one day... What else my enemies could have asked for me?

It was midnight and Mayank was sitting with me, besides a move 'n shift 'Pappu's shop' and having his Maggie. The call centre cabs were zipping past; reminding us of Star Wars spaceships; picking up aliens to and fro from their base stations and carrying them to their Mother Ships.

"So, now what have you thought, dude...?" Mayank asked, making recursive loops of Maggie around his plastic fork.

I was so lost and sad in my thoughts that he had to literally shake my legs to wake me up.

"What am I supposed to do *yaar*, so far destiny has kept on doing me, both ways." I replied exasperatedly.

"But you have got to do something man, I mean anything but sitting like this." His loop ended as the fork finally went back to his mouth.

"Mayank, easier said than done, tomorrow HR is going to release my termination letter sharp at 10:00. How much time do I have?" I got up to my feet and walked towards the road, hoping for one of the vehicles to change its route slightly and make my life easy.

There was a pause for another few minutes, that seemed like ages to me.

Suddenly Mayank crushed his plastic plate and threw it into the trash and said, "You know how I fool my girlfriends and make them do what I want?"

This is definitely not the time for your Casanova stories and all that crap, what's your problem, bragger?

I turned back angrily to face him and he raised his hands defensively as if trying to say, "Hang on dude, I mean business!"

My questioning eyes made him speak again, "See it's easy, I record all the mushy late night intimate talks of my bitches and edit them to make it look like a poor..."

I did everything but to have him by his lapels, "Mayank, I am not here to listen to your C grade stories, if you've got their recordings then do I have...?"

I stopped midway, realizing what I was actually saying ... realizing what Mayank was trying to point at ... his expression had suddenly changed to "See, I told you, I make sense!"

But my soaring spirits fell again, "No Mayank, it's not going to be easy, I mean I have a Handover-Takeover's recording, what can we do with that thing?" I kicked a pebble on the ground.

"Raj, you have got roughly an hour of his voice; I have got a rich and efficient skill set in putting apples and oranges together to make it look like grapes, rather sound like!"

I appreciated his bad PJ but would it be effective?

"Raj bro, this is what we guys do, we cut and copy different pieces of codes together to make it one logical one ... as long as it executes, who cares a shit?" came the next philosophical thought from Mayank.

Moreover, I didn't have much option, the worst was being kicked out of the organization and that was anyway going to happen with the coming daylight, what's the big deal?

"Ok Mayank, let us give it a fight before I go down..." I stood up, picking my helmet, as a gladiator about to enter the arena.

"Trust me dude, I have screwed up enough things to know how to fix screwed up ones...," Mayank stopped abruptly after seeing my depressed face.

"Lets get going chief!! We have a long night ahead and sadly I have to pass it with you, shit!" Finally he could make me smile.

As I rode on my bike and drove after him, a gush of chilled wind hit my body and so did a pang of sadness.

'Why the hell I am doing all this if Nayana is going … then what would I do with the job and my dreams?' My thoughts flashed one after another, faster than the trees zipping past.

But as my bike took the final turn, I thought, 'If we love each other, then she is going to come back to me, one fine day.'

Mayank was staying in Jia Sarai. A place as strange as it sounds for the first time. It's full of guys who are aspirants for the Public Services and, despite looking like a dingy and dark place, it produces enormous number of successful guys in PCS exams. More like Spidey's hideout, eh?

Mayank and I walked past a 'Tea - snacks' shop, which used to open at wee hours of the morning and close as the first ray of rising sun hit the world.

"I hope count Dracula is not running this shop!" I said in an attempt to lighten my mood as I took the flight of stairs to Mayank's room.

Mayank's room looked like the mini street of an Indian town during election campaigns - studded with all kind of animated poses of our great leaders and poll dancers. Well the poses here were quite animated too, but instead of leaders - here we had cheerleaders and pole dancers.

As he opened his mix and match recording application, it looked more like the dashboard of some spaceship. A number of freaky spiky red and green fluctuating waves aligned one after another and a lot of tuning buttons on the left bar, which Mayank started to play with swiftly.

"You are a geek man, what the hell are you up to?" I tried to comprehend the visual orchestra the coloured beams were playing around...........

"When it's driven by passion, it all becomes easy dude, now fast, give me the recording you have!"

We played the recording - fortunately it was crystal clear as it started running. Unfortunately I had to listen to the "not so soothing now" voice of the sick bastard for a complete hour.

"The risk profile can be drawn out in 3 easy steps..."

"Without this factor, all data is meaningless and stupid ... Bet your butt on that..."

"The heavy mail attachments get swapped by lighter HTML formats..."

"The development would take days and nights of effort ... take it easy man, you have enough time."

"The thin client base ensures a global roaming access … Raghav and Mayank know it better."

"This feature ensures security against theft and hacking attacks..."

"Raj, How did you know that already…? You almost stole my words, man." I was almost pukish to hear my name from that Ass.

"The front end may not end up being too artistic … Who cares anyway…?". It was bad to hear my name from him.

"QPM is the most vital assignment in the pipeline…"

Never in our life (IT one) we had toiled so hard to put the staggered and scattered pieces of code together as we did in that hell of a night. I was amazed to see Mayank's zeal and efficiency at his "manipulative work" - which he used till date only to lure lasses into his not so pure love stories.

We slept at 5:00 in the morning - Only to be woken up by the milkman after 2 hours with an infinite loop of palm strokes on the door laden with posters of Pamela Anderson.

Chapter 19: Payback Time

Mayank and I sat at the end of the UFO shaped meeting table – with the not-so-cool looking "black circled eye" alien visages.

"Do you think he's going to walk into this trap man?" – I asked nervously, fidgeting around with my mobile, just to ensure that my mind gets distracted from my numb and shaky fingers.

"A back stabber would never know what went on behind his back – would he? Besides, do we have options?" He said as his eyes slowly followed a dust particle, dancing in the morning sun ray.

My drowsy mind couldn't tail his thought nor the flying rolling stone.

Suddenly the glass door opened with a swift movement. The stained image which surfaced from behind the glass door sent a sick and cold chill down my gut.

"You guys called me in here, that too on your last day … Mr Worm – a…" He raped my surname with all his sky-high ego.

"Sundeep, we are sorry for our mistake to underestimate your abilities to hit below the belt." Came back the hiss from Mayank.

"You bloody *%$! Outcasts… Standing on the edge of the cliff and still have the cheek to talk to me this way." His fat body started having vigorous vibration with anger and disdain.

"See bro..." Unfazed Mayank was actually trying to poke the bully, and he was going great guns.

"You sucked up on our energies and working while pretending to suck something else."

Now he stepped forward and stood between me and Sundeep, I was not sure whether he did that to offend the fat pig or to hide my perspiring forehead.

"I know it's our farewell day, but we want to give you a small gift before we leave." I was happily consoled to say "we" instead of my name only.

"Have you two gone nuts...?" I could see the transforming face and voice of Sundeep, from anger to frustration and then to hues of sarcasm and sadism.

"Call it what you want it, but we want you to get the parting gift from us... We won't take much of your precious time." I said coming forth, Mayank's calmness was now lifting my spirits as well.

"Madmen – that's what you losers have turned into," he chuckled – Now enjoying the pain and frustration he had put us through.

"So you don't want to "hear" the parting gift of ours for you ... Mr Sand-deep?" Mayank's arrows of puns were still darting through.

But the Ostrich wasn't affected – "Hear? Have you got me a self-recorded crying opera guys?"

"You are so good at reading minds Sandeep – The way you read mine to capture the entire QPM thing." I tried my best to keep my fists from crash landing on the pig's nose.

"Ah, you are a heart-burnt kid ... still trying to manage your sent and draft emails?" Sundeep was far away from being "shame-dip".

"You guys can settle your score later – Lets hear the whining opera first." Mayank pressed my shoulder and pulled me back. This wasn't the time.

We sat down, not like the prettiest looking trio.

"Let's hear the IT idles' lullaby". Sundeep sang along, as Mayank navigated to his mobile's recording section.

As he pressed the "play" button – A chill went down my spine, If this fails, we can go to jail as well – leave alone a pink slip.

The clip started with a dance number playing along – I wasn't too happy with Mayank's creativity bit.

However, Sundeep's cheap mind was entirely animated and amused by this as his tapping fingers and toes confirmed that.

"I am loving it guys – hope I can take this gift back home?" – Where did you get this idea from anyhow?"

We sat in complete silence – waiting for the key part to get played along.

And it started...

"Do you like this kind of song – Sundeep...?." Mayank's voice abruptly drowned out the song's glitterati.

"When was this?" The toe tapper froze to almost a numb idol – hearing the unexpected twist in the tale...

"Hard party boozing hits the memory retention powers – especially the day to day ones..." Prof. Duggal spoke, Gently folding back his sleeves.

I was praying hard in my mind – Is Mayank being over confident? – If the Pig sniffs it, that would be a disastrous end to it.

The recording played on...

"Oh yes – you bet your butt on that - ...coz..." ... Sundeep was flowing along in his "daru-logues".

"When did I say that shit – this is all so untrue..." The tapping fingers got together and slammed down the table.

This was the defining moment, like a dangling bus on the edge of a cliff – a feather's weight was enough to topple it down or to put it back on ground.

I didn't let my anxiety surface in my eyes or face. Carefully watching the pig who wasn't quite enjoying the mud coming his way.

"I know Mr Cheater – A fake and thief's voice can sound fake only." Mayank spat out his well chewed and rehearsed words – leaning forward on the table.

There was more fun coming our way...

"But Sandeep, you shouldn't have done this thing with my QPM project..." – I was almost begging in the night old recorded version.

The Piglet's frozen face turned back to the recording screen – As If trying to exorcise the "whodunit" ghost out of it.

But in the magical not-so-idiot gadget it was incessantly rolling on...

"Take it easy man, there is a thin line between theft and artistic skills, right?"

The pig was perspiring ... two big beads of sweat rolled down from behind his ears and two other big ones quickly replaced them in no time.

"How did you do this Sundeep? – I mean this all sounds like a cock and bull story..." This was my unchained whining again. I just hoped that he didn't catch my drowsy yawn in that line.

But Sundeep was much too deep into the booby trap to see the small loopholes. The expressions on his face, cupped in his throbbing fingers, was "Am I about to spoil it all?"

And he heard that he had blown it from what followed:

"Easy steps ... Simple hacking to account of Raghav, stole QPM presentation and placed to make Raj feel as if Mayank did all the dirty work…"

"Ha…Ha….Haa… Am I not great guys?"

"This last laughter act was awesome..." Loved to see the monster coming out of you. Mayank paused the recording. Almost like taking an intermission break.

"You)$*))$ asses. How are you going to prove this is authentic?" Sundeep sprang up on his legs, which were shaking now, like his shallow confidence…

"We can't do that … It's up to Raghav, Ganesh and Rahul to take a call…" I eased back into my chair and played blind. Little were the other options to go with.

"…" We didn't hear any squealing or head butt attacking gestures from Sundeep. His eyes were wide open in amazement; lips had dried up like ash and stayed ajar for what felt like an eternity.

I was still trying to fathom which way the feather is tipping off the bus.

"All right, so shall we start hearing your next confession story Sir?" Mayank crossed over his legs and smirked back at Sundeep.

Next?? There was no next recording, this was it. I swung back my neck at Mayank but quickly ironed out my face of all the emotions it was going through.

"What the hell are you talking about?" Sundeep tried his best to settle his sweaty palms on the cold wood of the table.

"Well – your artistic story-telling about how you dug a hole for Raj with all your sick allies -- Tushar and whosoever else -- to drag him into this mess." Mayank's thumb was only a whisker away from playing it.

I swear to God I was shaking and trembling from inside, as nervous as Sundeep was if not more than him.

The feather was about to save or doom the bus. Fly my way baby.

The next passing second saw an unbelievable "Sundeep sprint" from the other side of the table to ours. He leaped and jumped to flash in front of us. Wow, that would surprise Neo in any part of matrix.

We responded and stood up quickly, ready to face anything coming from him, be it a spit or a hit.

"Guys, please save my ass..I'd do anything you say…".The eyes which were still wide open; were now pouring out the century's worst rainfall.

The transformation was magical, from Neo to Nirupa Roy in just a few seconds.

His knees almost gave in and he collapsed on all four – The sun was finally dipping deep down for Sundeep.

We turned our heads towards each other. Relived more than happy that he didn't ask for the rest of the recording played.

"Rise Sundeep." Mayank commanded, sounding no less than any King of Kings Mother Earth had ever seen.

He somehow mustered his all staggering body and soul into one bunch and wiped his forehead and face off sweat and tears.

"We need you to go and explain to Rahul all the nasty things you have been up to. We would talk it over again with him to see that this matter doesn't go out of this office."

He nodded his head in complete silence and agreement. Boy, I was loving it.

As he stepped back to the door to go out and think over the storm that just overtook him, I galloped and spat away my vengeance dialogue I had rehearsed at least a million times in my head.

"I agree that it's a jungle out here but Even the jungle has some rules, Sandy… If one fine day a wolf in sheep's clothing decides to be the George of the Jungle, it doesn't mean that he can dethrone the Lion, did you get that?" I roared back at him.

The state of mind he was in, it hardly could pinch him anymore. He kept on dragging himself outside the room.

"What the hell did that filmy stuff mean, Raj?" Mayank loomed over me with a questioning face.

"I don't know and I don't care, I am just happy that I am going to get what I deserved in life…"

"Right mate, QPM is and always was your baby." Mayank was happy to see me relieved.

"I am not talking about QPM, I am talking about my good old buddy Mayank who I doubted and shouted at so much." I pressed his arms tightly. "Would you please forgive me?"

"That's going to cost you 3 extra beers tonight… Deal?" He grinned and bared his big smile.

We hugged each other tight and walked back to our cubicles … and we walked real tall!

There was another QPM kudos party thrown that night. There Sundeep sat in a corner, sipping on his lemonades and trying to hide the books he had bought from the store in the evening.

Ganesh told us the next day that the book's name was *Memory Retention in Late Thirties* and *How to Regain what Alcohol Snatched from You.*

"Why would he be reading such books after such shameful acts?" He asked us curiously.

"No Idea Sir..." We shrugged our shoulders and smiled -- the smiles which turned into chuckles on the way and exploded into uncontrollable laughter once we went back to our cubicles.

Chapter 20: Life Offline

A week after the QPM going live, my life had again come back to a standstill.

Although it was fun -- getting my old buddy back, laughter, respect, and, to top it all, the late night boozing in the highway *dhabas*.

But something was missing.

I was missing Nayana. And I was being too pseudo stubborn to not accept this.

It was one of those lazy winter mornings when I walked to the "cost cutting" coffee vending machine. This machine delivered an efficient 10:90 ratio of milk and water with the latter always tending to go up.

And I couldn't help getting caught up in her thought as I slid the handle-less cup inside the nozzle.

"Her eyes ... lips ... the tousles playing on and around her face and her smile which..."

"Hey dude, what do you think you are up to...?" I was woken up to reality by a vigorous shake on my shoulder. It was Mayank.

"You have spoiled almost half the milk, while you were lost in your thought's milky way." I heard a murmur from one of the girls queued up for the economic coffee.

"Shit…" I cursed myself and realized that I had burnt my fingers with the milk spilling out.

"Before these angry guys milk you in the wrong way … Let's get out of here." Mayank grabbed my jacket and pulled me away.

"Let's go to CP and kill some time…" Mayank quipped as I was trying to air cool my ailing thumb.

"CP?.Why the hell to CP and what about office?" I was surprised, happy and then confused with the whole idea.

"Because my dear, *Badshah* Akbar's hall of commons and special is close and besides, do you have any real work here?" Mayank raised his eyebrows and shrugged his shoulders.

"No... Not really... But what do we tell Ganesh?" I was still possessed by the kindergarten spirit. Don't leave the classes till the last bell rings.

Mayank, as If reading my thought, said "Write a half day leave application to the class teacher Ganesh." Mayank giggled and chuckled backed at my kid-like behaviour.

I smirked back and sheepishly texted Ganesh with the age old excuse of being "under the weather" and hit the road on our way to CP.

The winter sun tried to shine with all its meek powers, like the sweet undercurrents of my feelings for Nayana.

Gosh, why can't I think of anything else, man?

We parked the bikes at the Janpath McD, destiny has its own strange ways to make you feel sad, happy and most of the times – "strange".

This was the place where I first met the lady of my thoughts, if not dreams.

"Hey, is she Suparna?" Mayank almost threw me out of balance with his push as I was busy taking the parking slips.

"Who Suparna? What are you sayin...?" How would I anyway know or remember when there are so many of them.

"Hey dude, Just hang on a second – I'll be back in a while." He dashed like a deer, sniffing the lush green meadow.

I was left alone again – and let myself settle on a corner table. Unknowingly or on purpose, this was again where we had sat together.

Is it really happening or you are giving some weird signs – I looked up and exhaled a big "I give up".

I still didn't know why I was acting so nostalgic and love-struck but I just kept on walking towards the sidewalk where we met for the first time.

I had no better way to kill time but to mock back at destiny in its very same way.

I pulled out my mobile and I played on a recording in the "Nayana" folder.

This was the one which she had recorded for me on my birthday, as her birthday gift for me.

"Raj... If God could fold and wrap all my dreams into one gift pack and send it to me from heavens, that would be him!"

Life had always been a game for me... However, I always ended up on the losing side of the table and the harder I tried to turn the wheel of fate, greater was the pain that life gave me... Breakups, back-stabbings and betrayals were the gory chapters of the black book of my life before I met him.

He is like an angel, and he was actually dressed like one when I met him J; a cream jacket, blue jeans and a white Tee... But what stole my heart were his eyes ... as pure as innocence and as playful as a kid's. I could never believe that someone can be this good and yet so amazingly all yours.

He washes away all my anger and frustration with just one soft peck and one bear hug. My short temper really scares the shit out of anyone. But he really knows every nerve in my body, the harder I scream and abuse him when fanatic and crazy, the broader is the smile he would flash and I always land in his arms, the place where I belong. The words that came out of my mouth when I saw him were...

"Where have you been all these days and years... Had I met you earlier, I wouldn't have had scars on my life..."

He never plans in his life, lives for the day and never minds if people just use him like a stepping stone to move ahead in life. He still thinks that it was destined to happen so it went that way. I am just the opposite and may be this is the reason why we complement each other so beautifully. I can never marry another "me", please for God's sake, else all hell would break loose on earth.

Life has never been the same all the way for anyone and we also faced the harsh realities of it which made us stay away from each other for quite long. We missed so much each other that we fought, cribbed and cried over the phone. But thankfully we never accepted it. He made my life so beautiful by just entering into it and being always there for me like my life support system. The more I think of him, the more I miss him and well ... I just love being lost in this loop.

Raj, please be the way you are. Why should we compete and compare with each other? Can't we just fall back and get lost into the innocent and childlike reverie we started our affair with. You are an angel, my God and I worship you. You make lives beautiful with your touches and smiles. Don't spoil your soul by getting into this rat race and even worse, trying to win it. You are not any other lesser mortal. You are my pride and my life and I would never let you down or feel low. Why can't we be just each other's support system? Why it has to be your or my life? Why can't it simply be OUR LIVES honey?

I love you and can't even think about anyone else. My God knows this and I would always wait for you to come like a knight in shining armour to kiss his princess.

I just want to say one thing that I always told you and that I always would keep on telling you and would love to scream to the whole world

I LOVE YOU…

I Love You…

I love you…

I love you…

The voice got choked and even my cell's recorder mocked my loneliness as it got stuck at the last sentence of "I love you."

"Damn it…" I glared back at my cell. "C'mon, have you had your share of laugh after listening to the gag that destiny was playing on me??"

But the recording had already ended; what is happening? Have I already started listening to voices as the after effects of the break off.

Then I felt a familiar touch on my shoulders and the hint of a scent which I knew better than my own body's.

And I couldn't believe that she actually came and sat next to me.

'Now have I even started seeing her everywhere after listening to her echoes?'

"I said I love you… Don't you feel like saying something Mr Raj?" She said, stone faced.

"But you left for the US. That's what you wrote…" I said, trying to control my choking voice.

"And you are so cool about it… I knew it ... I had doubts but now I know for sure that you are seeing someone. You did not even ask me why I was going and would I ever be back?"

"You think so small about me, I left for US and this was 'you and I *wala* US' and not United States of A…"

"…" I was speechless as my tongue was lying dead in the warm coffin of my mouth.

"And here you are… Waiting for the new lady in your life… OR are you just celebrating your independence day at the same place where we met?"

Was she just teasing me or was she deeply hurt?

"No... Nayana ... I actually got so caught up in a mess that you have no idea what state of mind I have been in…" I tried to carefully gauge her reaction, whether it was her mock tease or was she really hurt?

"Look Raj, I stayed away as I wanted to see if you really needed me." Her voice was soothing down to normal pitch now.

"I wish I could tell you how much I missed you Nayana. It was just that…" I fell short of words to explain my state of mind.

"I was just an email away Raj, but you didn't ever try … You don't want me -- I think." Her choking voice again put my tongue back in the mortal state.

"Ok, If this is what you want, I guess I should let you wait for the princess of your dreams!!" She turned her back on me, wiping her tears with the back of her palm.

I had almost lost so many things within the last few days that I just couldn't imagine a single moment of life without she being a part of it.

I quickly jumped past her, taking her in my arms, and gently whispered into her ears, "What if I say that the princess is right in front of my eyes and I never want this beautiful dream to end!"

"Then I think I can change the capital punishment into a life imprisonment, but only if you agree to share the cell on a twin sharing basis. Do you like that?" She took my palms in hers.

"I think I would love that, let's get started with the Day 1." I pulled her close.

"So, I hope the recording you were hearing of me was genuine and you didn't doctor it." She took a step back and winked at me.

"What, how the hell did you...?" I was surprised and shocked to my best of wits.

"That would be me, Sire." It was Mayank who jumped in front of us out of nowhere.

"Yes Raj, it was he who kept us connected, thanks to his hi-tech spying devices." They were chuckling back at me now.

"Man, so this day off, CP and McD was all part of your plan?" I owed two to Mayank now.

"Whatever..." Mayank shrugged off his shoulders as if this was no big deal for him. "By the way, it was Richa and not Suparna and I really need to go after her."

He dashed away again as we waved him off, smiling and content.

On the way, we crossed an internet cafe. Though it was an invasion of privacy, my eyes glued on one of the chat windows on the screen.

2Hot2Handle: Hi, I am Ravi, 26/m, a S/W engineer, your a/s/1 please.

Ragini_da_Mystery: Hi I am Ragini, 27/f, I am a S/W engineer, nice chat name!!!!

2Hot2Handle: Thanks, I guess you would have the same opinion about me as well. Wanna dig more?

Ragini_da_Mystery: Well you sound interesting, let's meet this Sunday morning...

"What happened?" Nayana shook my hands and asked me.

"Nothing, let's move..." I flashed a content smile and made her head rest on my arm.

Sometimes life seems so much better on our side of the line.